"Sometimes I feel as if there's a war going on inside me," Dane said. "One part of me's trying to forget. The other part's trying to remember...."

"Both sides will make peace with each other," Maria told him softly as his head lowered to hers, "but you have to let them."

His lips met hers with a demand greater than any she'd ever felt from him. She wasn't prepared for this passion, this wanting.

But the wanting stopped her. Did Dane simply want an escape from his past?

The question brought a dose of reality that Maria had to face. She backed away from him, still trembling from the desire that had pushed them together and was now tearing her apart. "I'd better go," she said quickly.

"Maria..."

Before he could say anything more, she turned, opened the door and stepped outside—and maybe out of his life....

Dear Reader,

I'm dreaming of summer vacations—of sitting by the beach, dangling my feet in a lake, walking on a mountain or curling up in a hammock. And in each vision, I have a Silhouette Romance novel, and I'm happy. Why don't you grab a couple and join me? And in each book take a look at our Silhouette Makes You a Star contest!

We've got some terrific titles in store for you this month. Longtime favorite author Cathie Linz has developed some delightful stories with U.S. Marine heroes and *Stranded with the Sergeant* is appealing and fun. Cara Colter has the second of her THE WEDDING LEGACY titles for you. *The Heiress Takes a Husband* features a rich young woman who's struggling to prove herself—and the handsome attorney who lends a hand.

Arlene James has written over fifty titles for Silhouette Books, and her expertise shows. *So Dear to My Heart* is a tender, original story of a woman finding happiness again. And Karen Rose Smith—another popular veteran—brings us *Doctor in Demand*, about a wounded man who's healed by the love of a woman and her child.

And two newer authors round out the list! Melissa McClone's *His Band of Gold* is an emotional realization of the power of love, and Sue Swift debuts in Silhouette Romance with *His Baby, Her Heart,* in which a woman agrees to fulfill her late sister's dream of children. It's an unusual and powerful story that is part of our THE BABY'S SECRET series.

Enjoy these stories, and make time to appreciate yourselves in your hectic lives! Have a wonderful summer.

Happy reading!

Mary-Theresa Hussey

Mary-Theresa Hussey
Senior Editor

Please address questions and book requests to:
Silhouette Reader Service
U.S.: 3010 Walden Ave., P.O. Box 1325, Buffalo, NY 14269
Canadian: P.O. Box 609, Fort Erie, Ont. L2A 5X3

Doctor in Demand

KAREN ROSE SMITH

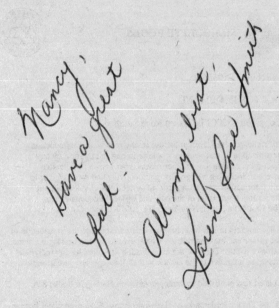

Nancy,
Have a great
fall!

All my best,
Karen Rose Smith

SILHOUETTE *Romance*

Published by Silhouette Books

America's Publisher of Contemporary Romance

To Carolyn Greene—Thanks for teaching me the power of brainstorming. But most of all, thanks for your friendship and support. Love, Karen.

I'd also like to thank Dr. Stephen Clancy for answering my medical questions so patiently and thoroughly.

 SILHOUETTE BOOKS

ISBN 0-373-19536-2

DOCTOR IN DEMAND

Copyright © 2001 by Karen Rose Smith

Visit Silhouette at www.eHarlequin.com

Printed in U.S.A.

Books by Karen Rose Smith

Previously published under the pseudonym Kari Sutherland

KAREN ROSE SMITH

is a former teacher and home decorator. Now spinning stories and creating characters keeps her busy. But she also loves listening to music, shopping and sharing with friends as well as spending time with her son and her husband. Married for thirty years, she and her husband have always called Pennsylvania home. Karen Rose likes to hear from readers. They can write to her at P.O. Box 1545, Hanover, PA 17331.

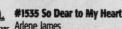

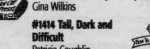
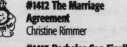
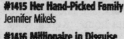

Chapter One

The New Mexico landscape should have captured Dane Cameron's interest. He'd been to the Southwest once before to attend a medical conference, but he hadn't seen much more than the inside of the hotel. Now that trip seemed like centuries ago—when he'd had a life filled with the work he loved...a wife...a son...

Although it was almost 5:00 p.m., a fiery sun burned in the turquoise sky. Following the directions the motel clerk had given him, Dane drove through the small town of Red Bluff, passing the sheriff's office, going through the town square and then a few blocks beyond. On the right he saw the sign for the Red Bluff Clinic and he turned into the parking lot. There were two vehicles there—a Jeep and a sedan.

He hoped the clinic was still open. He was eager to get a glimpse of the place where he'd be working. It was an eagerness that was almost a surprise after the numb, mechanical, going-through-the-motions kind of existence he'd led for almost two years.

As he strode to the front door of the clinic he noticed the landscaping, so different from what he was used to in the Northeast. The lawn, if you could call it a lawn, was mostly gravel, cactus and some brush topped with tiny purple flowers. But as he reached the door of the building, he was more interested in what he would find inside.

The vibrancy of the reception area struck him first with its Spanish and Native American motifs evident in everything from the paintings on the walls to the pottery on a bookshelf to the string of chilies hanging on an inside door. Burgundy and dark green dominated the furnishings with splashes of blue thrown in here and there. As he stopped at the receptionist's window, he saw that the small cubicle was empty.

The door decorated with chilies was hanging open, and Dane thought he heard voices from that direction. Following the sound, he paused outside of an examining room where the door stood ajar. When he glanced inside, he suddenly halted in his tracks. There was an older woman standing by the sink.

But it was the second, younger woman in a white lab coat with a stethoscope around her neck who drew his gaze. She was speaking in a low voice to her patient. What had stopped him was her exotic beauty. Her hair was the color of lush sable. Drawn into a ponytail, it fell halfway down her back. Her cheekbones were high and finely sculpted, her nose straight, her chin delicately defined. Her skin was tan, her breasts high and full, her hips softly curved under the cotton of her white coat.

He remembered Maria Youngbear's throaty contralto voice over the phone, how he'd wondered what she'd look like. If this was the doctor he'd be working with...his body was giving off signals that hadn't been part of his life for a very long time.

Before Dane could absorb the impact of feeling sexual desire again, there was suddenly a commotion in the waiting room. Someone from there yelled, "Dr. Youngbear! Come quick."

Knowing an emergency when he heard it, Dane started back to the reception area and found two men in gray uniforms. The younger of the two, who was probably in his late twenties, had red splotches on his face and arms. His lips were swelling.

His partner said quickly in explanation, "Wasps got him. He said his throat was getting tight."

Although Dane was a pediatric cardiologist, he remembered his rotation in emergency medicine. On a quick, cursory examination, he ascertained the man was having an anaphylactic reaction.

"I'm Dr. Cameron," he told the two men, showing them quickly down a hall to an empty examination room.

With the sound of voices, Maria Youngbear had stepped into the hall. Her gaze passed quickly over Dane—his tan polo shirt and khaki slacks. Then her attention focused on the man who'd been stung. "Rod! What happened?"

Before the young man could try to answer, Dane said tersely, "Dane Cameron. We've got a patient with multiple stings. I need subcutaneous epinephrine as well as IM Benadryl—stat."

Maria's eyes were deep-brown with specks of amber. They widened only a moment, then went back to the man with the splotches. "I'll get what you need," she said to Dane in a rush.

By the time Dane instructed Rod to lie on the table in the exam room, Maria was back with syringes.

Dane took them from her and cursed the fingers on his right hand which still wouldn't bend properly. Over the past six months since he'd decided to accept this position in Red Bluff, he'd become somewhat ambidextrous, but it was still awkward. After wiping Rod's arm with an alcohol swab he found in a jar on the counter, he injected the medication.

Grabbing the stethoscope Maria had stuffed into her pocket, Dane attached it around his neck. For the next fifteen minutes he examined and monitored Rod carefully. The swelling had stopped and the deputy's face wasn't quite so red.

Dane gave the young man another injection, then clasped his shoulder. "How are you feeling?"

The patient grimaced. "Better. My throat's not tight anymore. The stings hurt like hell, though."

"We'll put cold compresses on the stings. You'll need to stay here till tomorrow so we can keep an eye on you. Unless you'd rather I call an ambulance to take you to the hospital."

As Dane remembered from the information Maria Youngbear had sent him, there wasn't a hospital in town. Rod would have to be transported to Albuquerque.

"No hospital," Rod muttered. "I'd rather stay here."

"Is he going to be all right?" Wyatt Baumgardner, the other man in uniform asked.

"You got him here in time. He should be fine by tomorrow."

Maria, who had been watching Dane as well as Rod, now asked tersely, "Dr. Cameron, may I see you out in the hallway?"

Dane studied her again. She *was* beautiful. "Sure." He said to Rod, "I'll be right back."

Out in the hall Maria looked up at him. "You obviously know how to take charge, Dr. Cameron, and that's a necessary quality in emergency medicine. But before you take over my clinic again, I'd appreciate it if you would consult with me. I have a patient to see. After I finish I'll give you a tour of the facility. Unless, of course, you decide to do the touring on your own. Joan's a registered nurse. She can get you anything you might need until I'm free." Then Maria Youngbear disappeared into the room next to Rod's and closed the door.

Dane stood there a few moments, not knowing what to make of the pretty doctor. She was obviously ticked off at him. For handling a crisis situation?

He'd never had the reputation some of his colleagues did for believing he could walk on water. He knew his limitations all too well, and he respected anyone who had worked with him to help him save a child's life. If Maria Youngbear expected him to consult with her on every move he made, she'd hired the wrong doctor.

A half hour later, after Wyatt had left with a friendly handshake and a welcome to the area, Rod had filled Dane in on Red Bluff, from the sheriff's department to the town council to the churches.

The opening of a door and then voices in the hall alerted Dane that Maria was finished with her patient.

When Joan came into the exam room, she said,

"Dr. Youngbear is free now. I can keep an eye on Rod."

With a nod, Dane checked Rod again, then left him under the nurse's watchful eye.

The door to the corner office was open and Maria Youngbear sat at one of the desks there, her head bent as she made notes. She'd shed her lab coat and her silky ponytail lay enticingly over her red knit top.

When she looked up, Dane asked, "Wouldn't it be easier to use a tape recorder?"

"Not unless I want to transcribe the notes as well as dictate them."

"Your secretary can't—"

"I don't have a secretary, Dr. Cameron. Betsy Fulton is my receptionist. The patients, as well as billing and scheduling their appointments, keep her busy. I do have a nurse-practitioner but she's out on maternity leave, and Joan is filling in until she returns." She motioned to the other desk in the room. "That's your desk."

At a glance he took in the space with its two desks, black leather sofa, bookshelves and file cabinet. "We're sharing an office?"

She leaned back in her chair then and studied him. "This isn't a big-city clinic. Our space is limited. If you need a private office, maybe you came to the wrong place."

As they gazed at each other in silent appraisal, Dane was aware of two things. Maria Youngbear affected him in a way a woman hadn't for a very long time. But she was angry with him, and he was beginning to understand why. This was her territory and he'd encroached upon it. She was ruffled because he'd usurped her power. Maybe that had happened too many times before.

"I didn't come to Red Bluff for a private office. As I explained in our phone interview, I came here for a change. If I stepped on your toes earlier, I didn't mean to, but I'm not going to apologize for acting quickly in a situation that needed it."

Her dark eyes widened a little in surprise at his blunt honesty, but then she gave him a rueful smile and extended her hand. "Why don't we start over? I'm Maria Youngbear. Welcome to Red Bluff."

He, too, extended his right hand and knew she felt the stiffness of his fingers when she shook it.

During their interview, he'd explained he'd been in an accident and had sustained damage to his right hand, but he'd assured her he could cover with his left. She'd seemed eager to sign him on in spite of that, telling him they could work around his injury.

"As I told you, I can use my left hand almost as well as my right," he assured her again. "In the operating room I needed both. In a family clinic, I'll manage just fine."

"Did you have physical therapy?" she asked, seeing the obvious scar from his fingers to below his wrist.

"I had surgery. That was enough." He hoped she'd realize it was a subject he didn't want to discuss. The accident that had taken his wife and son and cost him his career was closed territory.

But Maria Youngbear apparently wasn't a woman who took a hint. "You don't want to practice pediatric cardiology again?"

"I took this job to practice as a general practitioner, and that's what I'm going to do."

When Maria had studied Dane Cameron's impeccable résumé over six months ago and interviewed him, he'd told her he wanted to come to Red Bluff to make a change in his life. Although her innate curiosity had wanted details, she'd respected his privacy and hadn't asked for them. After all, he was the find of the century as far as she was concerned. Her notice in a medical newsletter had only produced one other response, and as soon as that young physician had heard the salary, he'd decided he wasn't interested. Dane Cameron, on the other hand, didn't seem to care about the money, just the work. Now that she'd met the man, she realized his wanting to change the focus of his career was only the tip of the iceberg.

As she looked into Dane's blue eyes, she felt transfixed by the deep turbulence stirring there.

With difficulty she tore her gaze from his and glanced at her watch. She was going to be late picking up her daughter from her mother's ranch. Thank goodness her parents understood physicians' hours. Thank goodness at two years old, Sunny only cared about being with people who loved her, and Maria's sometimes upside-down schedule didn't seem to affect her. As Maria often did, she thanked the Lord for Sunny, who'd been a welcome gift from a marriage that had failed miserably before it had much chance to start.

"I can give you a brief tour of the clinic if you'd like," she said to Dane. "But then I must be going. I have to pick up my daughter and get us both ready for Dr. Grover's retirement party this evening. He's the physician you're replacing. Joan is going to stay overnight to watch over Rod. I'll call periodically to see how he's doing, and she can page me if she needs me."

"I can stay," Dane offered.

Maria wondered if he was that dedicated or just restless after his arrival in a new town. "Your official starting date isn't until Monday. It will keep our paperwork in order if we stick to that." The reality was she needed time to absorb his presence, to get used to the idea of working beside this handsome doctor.

After studying her long enough to make her feel uneasy and all too aware of him, Dane threw her off guard. "How old is your daughter?"

The thought of Sunny brought a smile. "She's two years, three months."

Dane's gaze went to Maria's left hand that was devoid of rings.

"I'm divorced." She didn't know why it was important to put that into words, but it was.

After a few moments of silence, when she seemed much too conscious of Dane's six-two height, of his terrifically broad shoulders, his thick blond hair, his very blue eyes, he said, "The tour of the clinic can wait till Monday. It'll be fairly easy to find my way around. Do you have a schedule of office hours?"

Maria suddenly felt at a disadvantage, sitting while Dane was standing. She instinctively knew that sharing an office with him would be much different from sharing one with Dr. Grover. There was an intensity about Dane Cameron that seemed to make the air all around him crackle.

She told herself she'd simply been putting in too many long hours, that Dane Cameron wasn't her type, that she wasn't curious to know a lot more about him.

Riffling through papers in a basket on her desk, she

plucked one from the container and stood. "This is our schedule."

When Dane took the paper from her hand, his thumb brushed against her palm. Tingles skipped up her spine, and she tried to ignore them.

But his gaze met hers, and ignoring anything that happened between her and Dane Cameron seemed to be impossible. She searched for something useful to say and realized she'd been remiss in not officially inviting him to Dr. Grover's Bon Voyage bash.

"Dr. Grover's party tonight is being held in the cafeteria of the elementary school if you'd like to come."

Tearing his gaze from hers, Dane quickly glanced at the hours on the sheet of paper and then stuffed it into the pocket of his khaki slacks. "I think I'll pass. I'm not a party person."

Something about Dane made her wonder if that had always been true. "I just thought it would be a good opportunity to introduce yourself to the patients of Red Bluff. This is a fairly small town, and everyone seems to know everyone else."

"And you think it would be good public relations if I'd attend," he stated rather than asked.

"I think it might help everyone become more comfortable with you."

He seemed to mull that over but didn't commit himself either way.

"If you decide to come, the party's at eight," she added. "The elementary school's on Rio. Where are you staying?"

"At the Sagebrush Motel. I'll need to find an apartment. Do you have any suggestions?"

Maria lived in an apartment complex a few blocks

from the clinic. The apartment adjacent to hers was vacant, but she didn't think she wanted to live next door to this good-looking doctor who stirred feelings in her that hadn't been stirred since before her divorce. It would be better to keep her distance if she could.

"Let me think about it. I'll make you a list."

He nodded. When he gave the office a last look, his gaze fell on the framed photograph atop Maria's file cabinet beside her desk. It was a picture of Sunny.

"Is that your daughter?" he asked.

There was a tightness in his voice and a look in his eyes that made her sense that looking at the picture was painful for him.

"It is," she said softly.

"She's beautiful."

Sunny's dark-brown eyes, slightly wavy chestnut hair, her sent-from-heaven smile always filled Maria with so much joy she couldn't keep from smiling herself. "Yes, she is. She's sugar and hope and everything good. I don't know what I'd do without her."

After Dane brought his gaze back to Maria's, she realized he suddenly looked much older than the forty years he'd claimed on his résumé. "I'll be on my way, then," he said tersely. "If I don't see you tonight, I'll be here around eight Monday morning. Will the clinic be open?"

"The receptionist comes in at eight. My first appointment is at nine."

Dane nodded, turned and then left her office. As he strode down the hall toward the reception area, Maria had the uncomfortable premonition that her life was going to become more complicated.

But she'd do her best not to let that happen.

* * *

It was almost 8:30 p.m. when Dane entered the elementary school cafeteria. He'd made a last-minute decision. Deciding to be a physician at the Red Bluff Clinic meant mingling with the townsfolk. As laughter, chatter and noise swirled about him, he told himself he'd come out of a sense of duty. Yet he found himself glancing over the crowd to see if he could spot Maria Youngbear.

Right away he realized he was overdressed in his navy dress slacks and white oxford shirt. He'd left his collar open, but after glancing around the room, he figured he'd better roll up his sleeves to make an attempt at looking casual. Lots of people wore shorts in deference to the July heat. Ceiling fans whirred, bobbing the helium balloons that were tied to many of the tables. A banner stretched across the side wall—Bon Voyage, Dr. Grover—and two tables near the front of the room held casseroles of food. There were two punch bowls and cups on another table and slices of chocolate and white cake on yet another. Residents of Red Bluff sat at the tables eating and talking while others mingled in groups here and there.

Dane felt adrift in a strange sea. He'd attended parties in New York, but not with the patients he'd treated. Most of them had been formal. Most of them had involved fund-raising. And Ellen had been by his side.

He strode toward the table with the punch. That would be a good place to start. He was halfway across the room when he caught a glimpse of luxuriant dark brown hair. Maria's hair was magnificent out of its ponytail. He studied her in her white peasant blouse embroidered with blue and red, the flowing, tiered,

red-blue-and-white-flowered skirt that brushed her ankles. He couldn't help but notice her red-painted toenails in the sandals that made her feet look delicate and very feminine. Everything about her shouted vibrancy and life. Did she affect him so because he'd secluded himself since the accident? Or was he intrigued with her because of the obvious differences between them?

As if she felt his gaze, she turned toward him, and their eyes met. For a moment he was immobilized as the air from the fan ruffled her bangs.

But then a child came running to her and wrapped her little arms around Maria's legs. Maria laughed and scooped up the little girl, then walked toward him.

He remembered holding Keith that way...he remembered too many things he'd tried desperately to forget.

Still, he couldn't take his eyes from the beautiful child. She was absolutely adorable in her yellow sundress with its ruffled sleeves and its teddy bear embroidered on the bodice. She wore tiny sandals no bigger than his palm, and his heart ached with a longing that would never go away.

Maria smiled up at him. "So you decided to come."

"The alternative was watching reruns on the motel TV," he responded wryly.

She laughed as her little girl laid her head on her mom's shoulder and stuffed her thumb in her mouth.

"What's her name?" Dane asked.

"Sunny."

Before he could comment on the unusual name, an older woman came up beside Maria. "Is this our new doctor?"

"Dr. Cameron, meet my mother, Carmella Eagle."

He extended his hand and shook hers.

An older man and a teenage boy now joined them.

Maria grinned broadly. "This is my father and my brother Joe."

Joe eyed Dane, sizing him up. His almost-black eyes weren't friendly.

Mr. Eagle also shook Dane's hand. "We're glad to have you here. Maria tells us your credentials are impressive. The town council took her recommendation to hire you without even a debate."

"Red Bluff Clinic is financed by a private foundation as well as town taxes," Maria explained. "That's why you had to be approved by the town council."

Dane's gaze seemed to gravitate to hers as if it didn't have anywhere else it wanted to go. "I can see I have a lot to learn about Red Bluff."

"Maybe you won't like small-town life," Joe said.

Dane thought he felt hostility from the teenager, but he couldn't understand why...unless Maria's brother sensed Dane's attraction to his sister. "I've never lived in a small town. This will be a change. But I'm hoping I'll learn to like it."

Maria's mother patted Dane's arm. "Maria will have to bring you for supper sometime soon. But now we have to get going. Tom and our eldest son are leaving early tomorrow morning to go to Santa Fe to look at some horses."

Carmella hugged and kissed her granddaughter. "See you on Sunday, little one." Then she hugged Maria, too. "Remember, Rita is bringing corn bread and Teresa is making dessert."

"I'll fix a salad," Maria said as she returned her mother's hug.

After goodbyes all around, Dane watched Maria's family move away. "Do you have a large family?"

"Three brothers and two sisters. We're a noisy bunch when we get together, especially with all of their children. My mother insists every Sunday is a holiday with the family there."

As Sunny curled once again on her mother's shoulder, chatter and noise filled the room. Yet somehow Dane felt as if he and Maria were standing there alone. She looked so soft and feminine with the puffed sleeves of her blouse, the scoop neck, her long flowing skirt.

"How long have you practiced here?" he asked, wondering her age, thinking she had a timeless beauty that made it impossible to tell.

"Four years. It was my first position after my residency."

"Do you ever want to practice anywhere else?" he asked, seeing how contented she seemed here.

"I thought about it before...before Sunny was born. But my family's here and so are my roots. Both mean a lot to me."

He'd had the feeling that she was about to say something besides "before Sunny was born." Maybe it had something to do with her marriage. Maybe it didn't. Either way, it was none of his business.

Dane's gaze drifted to Sunny again, and he saw that her eyes were almost closed. "I guess it's past her bedtime."

Maria smiled. "I have to get her home. But first let me introduce you to Dr. Grover. He'll be leaving on a cruise in a few days and won't be back for two months. He attempted to retire once before, but then circumstances brought him back and now he says nothing will postpone his retirement.''

In the next half hour Dane not only met Dr. Grover and his wife but several other residents of Red Bluff who were curious as to who he was. He felt like a goldfish, not only in a fishbowl, but out of water, too. For a long while now, he'd seemed to be set apart from everyone back home, as well. It was him—not where he was or who he was with.

Finally Maria said, ''I really do have to go. I want to stop at the clinic to look in on Rod.'' She shifted Sunny to her other shoulder where the little girl yawned.

''I'll walk you out,'' Dane said.

''Oh, that's not necessary. I know you want to mingle.''

''I can only take so much mingling in one evening.''

As Maria said final goodbyes to friends she passed on their way to the door, Dane thought how different this practice was going to be from what he was used to. He usually treated strangers. Once their case was finished, he never saw them again. But here in Red Bluff with a family practice, care continued throughout a patient's lifetime. It was something he never thought about before—knowing his patients. It was an odd concept.

Once outside, he realized the temperature had dropped and the air was almost cool.

When he started for the parking lot, Maria said, ''We walked. I'll see you Monday morning.''

He stopped. ''I'm not letting you walk to the clinic alone at night.''

"This is Red Bluff, Dr. Cameron, not New York City. We have a terrific sheriff's department."

"Terrific sheriff's department or not, I'll give you a ride to the clinic and then home."

"It's really not far."

He saw something in her eyes then, something that told him the stirring he felt for her when their gazes met might be reciprocated. It was so strange, the aliveness that seemed to be humming between them. He'd never felt that with Ellen. With her he'd experienced friendship, satisfaction, comfort.

He shouldn't be thinking about that now. Thoughts of Ellen would lead to thoughts of everything else. His nightmares had finally slowed to about one a week, and he didn't want to encourage them to resurface more often.

"She'll get heavier with each block you walk," he warned, nodding to Sunny. "Besides, she might get chilled in this night air."

After a pause Maria conceded, "You could be right about that. If you're sure you don't mind..."

"I don't mind." Inexplicably he wanted to prolong the evening and talk to Maria a little longer. Maybe because a spartan motel room waited for him.

He motioned to a white SUV that needed a good washing. He'd taken his time driving from New York to Red Bluff, seeing some sights along the way. He hadn't had anything better to do.

Opening the passenger side with his remote, he waited until Maria climbed in. Then he shut the door. She shouldn't be holding her little girl. Sunny should be in a car seat. But he knew even car seats couldn't always protect children. Nothing could.

They were at the clinic a few minutes later. When

Joan saw Sunny, she gathered her into her arms like a favorite aunt and took her to get a cartoon sticker while Maria checked on the deputy, whose wife of just a few months was keeping him company.

Dane looked around the clinic while Maria examined Rod. The facility wasn't large, but it was adequately equipped.

Twenty minutes later Maria was ready to leave. After a few last instructions to Joan, she gathered Sunny into her arms again and carried her to Dane's car. As he drove, she gave him directions, and they arrived at her apartment building in less than five minutes.

After Dane parked, he came around and opened Maria's door. "I'll take her for you," he said gruffly, knowing it would be easier for Maria to climb out.

Thank goodness it was dark. Thank goodness that sweet cherubic face was in shadows. It made it easier for him to take the toddler in his arms, to hold her a few moments until Maria closed her door. When Sunny tucked her head against Dane's shoulder, the gesture caused him so much pain, he sucked in a breath. He'd thought he'd become numb to it. He'd thought he'd become numb to almost everything.

He'd come to Red Bluff for a change, but he didn't know if he was ready for a reawakening until he heard himself say to Maria, "I'll carry her."

They walked the path along the building until he saw the sign that read Sierra Apartments and underneath spotted, Vacancy.

"Your building has apartments for rent?"

"Actually, the apartment next to mine is vacant. I was going to give you a list including that one. I didn't know what price range you were interested in."

"I just need someplace comfortable where I can crash at night."

The scent of Maria's perfume teased him in the still night as she led him under an arch and into a hallway. After she took out her key, she suggested, "If you want to come in for a few minutes, I'll show you the layout. If you're interested, you can contact the landlady tomorrow."

"I'd like that." He wanted to see where she lived, and he liked the idea of being close to her.

Once inside, Maria switched on the lights.

"Where would you like me to put her?" he asked.

Moving quickly, Maria showed him through a living room with comfortable-looking, light-blue and teal-green furnishings to a bedroom beyond. There were puffed and padded cloud hangings on the walls, a colorful rainbow and a white crib and chest.

"I'll take her now," Maria said, slipping her arms around her sleeping daughter.

Maria's hands grazed Dane's chest, and he looked down at her, swallowing hard. Though he needed to step back, though he knew distance between them was best, he also wanted to feel her touch again. And he imagined lacing his fingers in her hair and feeling the warmth of her lips under his. Maybe he'd driven too long in too short a time.

Her brown eyes avoided his as she laid Sunny in her crib, slipped off the tiny sandals and sundress and slid a nightgown over her head. Then she kissed her daughter on the cheek and murmured good-night.

His elemental reaction to Maria, her tenderness with her daughter, the simple nightly ritual of a kiss good-night made Dane's gut clench. He strode into the living room and then stopped and inhaled a deep breath.

When Maria joined him, she asked, "Would you like something to drink?"

Scotch on the rocks would be good, he thought, but even though he wasn't on call, he knew he needed a clear head right now. Thank God he'd only used alcohol for a short while to drown the pain. "No, thanks." He took a good long look around. "Are all of the apartments the same?"

"For the most part. There's a terrace. Some have three bedrooms instead of two, but essentially the floor plans are alike."

Maria's beautiful hair swept along her cheek and down her shoulder. The dim light in the living room made the atmosphere intimate, and kissing her seemed a very natural idea to contemplate.

Before he did more than just think about it, he moved toward the door. "I'd better be going. Thanks for letting me look around. I'll call the apartment manager tomorrow."

He was about to step over the threshold when Maria said, "Thank you for the ride home, Dr. Cameron."

Pausing, he turned back to look at her. "It's Dane, Dr. Youngbear."

She smiled. "It's Maria…Dane. Try to get a good weekend's rest. I'll be introducing you to a truckload of patients on Monday."

"It will be good to be working again."

There were questions in her eyes, questions he didn't want to answer, questions he had no intention of answering. Before the idea of kissing her gripped him even stronger, he said, "I'll see you on Monday."

Then he walked away.

Chapter Two

Juggling groceries in one arm and holding on to Sunny with her other hand, Maria stepped into the shade of her building's arched hallway, heading for her apartment. But before she got there, the door to the apartment next to hers opened and Dane came out.

She'd had a restless night's sleep last night remembering the color of his eyes and features of his face. Although she'd almost managed to banish them from her thoughts while she was running errands with Sunny, now...

Dane was smiling, and his smile did funny things to her insides as he held up a key. "We're going to be neighbors."

The groceries were getting heavier by the minute, and as Maria bent to set them at her door until she found her key, Dane was suddenly there in front of her, taking the bag from her.

"Here, let me help you with that."

"It's all right. I—"

His hand brushed her waist as he lifted the bag from her, and she felt flustered and tongue-tied and too much like a schoolgirl.

"You aren't used to accepting help, are you?" His blue gaze was insistently probing.

"That depends on the help," she answered flippantly, not knowing how else to cover the attraction she felt for this man. He was dressed in jeans and a red polo shirt today and was devastatingly handsome even in that.

Fishing in the pocket of her white shorts, she found her key and inserted it into the lock. As the door opened, Sunny raced inside ahead of her.

Maria turned to take the groceries from Dane, but he offered, "I'll carry them."

Sunny toddled to the sofa where some of her toys lay. Maria saw Dane's glance linger on her daughter.

"Why did you name her Sunny?" he asked.

Sunny's name had a special meaning to Maria, but she didn't know Dane well enough to tell him that her pregnancy was all that had kept her going for a while after her divorce, and she'd named her little girl as a sign of hope. She simply said, "I named her Sunny because I knew she'd brighten up my days. She has."

There was something in Dane's eyes then, something she'd glimpsed the evening before that led her to ask a question that now seemed very important. There had been no talk of a wife or a family on his résumé, nor in any of their conversations. He wasn't wearing a wedding ring.

"Have you ever been married?" she asked, knowing she was treading into personal territory.

"I'm a widower," he answered curtly, setting her

bag of groceries on the table in the dining area. Then he went to stand at the sliding glass doors that looked out over the back landscape. Changing the subject, he waved to the terrace that was adjacent to his. "I suppose I'll have to buy outdoor furniture. I didn't need that in New York."

Evidently the subject of his marriage was taboo. For now she'd let it be. "Are you having your furnishings shipped out here?"

He shook his head. "I sublet my apartment as is. I thought that was best until I made sure this job...worked out. I'll just get the necessities for now. Do you know a good place to buy furniture?"

Maria sensed that the road before Dane wasn't a straight one. He was finding his way, and he didn't know if living in Red Bluff was his future. "There are a few stores I particularly like." Then, realizing how it must feel to be in a strange place, knowing no one, she added, "I'm driving into Albuquerque later this afternoon. If you'd like to go along, I can show you around."

Dane turned away from the patio doors then, and his gaze fell on her face and then her lips. She could feel the heat from him, and her heart began pounding, though there was no reason for it to.

Suddenly Sunny came running from the sofa and tugged on Maria's shorts. "Juice, Mommee?"

The spell was broken. Stooping down, Maria picked up Sunny, holding her close in her arms, reminding herself of her life, telling herself Dane was a stranger who might not be staying in Red Bluff.

"Orange or cranberry?" she asked her daughter.

"Owange."

Dane's expression when he looked at Sunny almost

hurt Maria. It was so sad. "What would you do with Sunny if we went into Albuquerque?" he asked.

"I'd take her along. We're separated so much during the week that I like to spend every moment I can with her on the weekends."

"I can understand that." His voice was gruff, but his words were filled with an empathy that told her he did understand. Still, he turned down her offer. "I think it might be better if I explore Albuquerque on my own. I wouldn't want to put you to any trouble."

That was his way of declining her invitation, and she had the strong feeling he didn't want to be around her daughter. Maria had never been known for her shyness, and if he had a problem caring for children, she wanted to know why.

Lowering her daughter to the floor, she suggested, "Go ask your dolly if she wants orange juice or cranberry, and I'll get some for both of you."

After Sunny smiled up at her, she ran over to the sofa again.

"What is there about my daughter that makes you so uncomfortable? You were a pediatric cardiologist. Don't you like children?"

His jaw tightened until he finally responded, "I'd rather not discuss it."

"I think we'd better discuss it. There are a lot of children in my practice." She wasn't going to back down when quality of care for her patients was at stake.

"I won't have a problem treating the patients," he informed her with curt determination.

Walls had gone up around him that were steep and thick. Maria suddenly wanted to tear them down and help him with whatever was troubling him. "Dane, we're going to be working together—"

"Exactly. We'll be working together. That doesn't give you the right to pry into my life."

There was no logical reason why she should feel hurt by his words, but she did and she knew she'd better back off. "Fine," she said softly. "I'll remember that."

The consultation with her doll finished, Sunny appeared at Maria's feet again. "Dolly want owange."

Dane glanced down at Sunny once again. "I'd better be going. While I have some free time this weekend, I want to learn my way around."

"Red Bluff will be busier than usual tomorrow."

His attention fell once again on her. "How so?"

"The Great Chili Cook-off. It's a once a year event and we draw tourists. The square will be blockaded for arts and crafts and food stands."

"It sounds interesting. I might have to check it out," he said politely.

She had the feeling that he'd sooner leave the town early in the morning and come back when it was all over. But that was none of her business, either. As he crossed to her door, she asked, "When will you be moving in?"

"I'm not sure yet, but I'll let you know. I'll see you Monday morning."

"Monday morning," she repeated as Dane left her apartment and shut the door.

For the first time in a long time, Maria thought about her ex-husband. Dane was so different from Tony. Tony had been a doctor, too. They'd met in medical school and gravitated toward each other, probably because of their Cheyenne heritage. They seemed to have so much in common, and her parents had approved heartily when they'd gotten engaged. But Maria's bonds to her family were something Tony had never quite understood. They'd worked together at the clinic for a year until he'd decided he wanted something different from Red Bluff. He'd signed on with a medical project in Africa, insisting she join him.

But Maria couldn't leave everything she'd known and loved, and hadn't gone with him. They'd argued, and both had been angry. Still, when Tony had served her with divorce papers long distance, that had shaken her up. She'd realized she still loved her husband and she'd wanted their marriage to work, even if that meant she had to join him in Africa.

When she'd surprised him by flying there, they'd had a reunion all right...until she'd found he was involved with someone there. She'd returned home hurt and devastated only to discover a few weeks later that their last attempt to save their marriage had resulted in a pregnancy—a pregnancy Tony didn't want. A pregnancy Maria wouldn't terminate.

And now here was Dane Cameron backing off from her daughter.

It didn't matter. They'd merely be working together. They'd merely be colleagues. And she wouldn't wonder about his secrets nor tell him any of hers.

On Sunday Dane drove under an amazing blue sky. The country out here seemed to soothe him in a way the northeastern country couldn't. Maybe because it was so different. Maybe because it didn't carry any memories. Maybe because he was really ready to see the world around him again. For whatever reason, he put his windows down and let the dry heat and air envelop him. Driving without a purpose was new to him. He'd always been goal oriented. His parents had divorced when he was six, and he'd always felt he worked harder than most kids to make his parents proud. They'd both been supportive since the accident, but they couldn't make anything better.

Only *he* could do that.

After the accident he'd been in limbo until he realized his career as a pediatric cardiologist was over, at least in the operating room. For the next year he'd acted as a consultant, going through the motions, using his expertise, smiling when people expected him to, working like a robot or a man with no soul. Then he'd seen the advertisement in the medical newsletter and looked into this position in Red Bluff. For some reason the idea of practicing here had given him motivation again as he'd waited for his medical license to come through in New Mexico. Finally last month it had. Now here he was, exploring the desert and mesas and cliffs, hoping he could find a future to replace the past.

It was early evening when he drove back to Red Bluff and saw the sign for the chili cook-off. Instead of stopping at his motel, he drove as close to the square as he could get and parked. The main street was lined with vendors of every ilk. He heard music coming from the square—violins, guitars, a tambourine. Strings of colored lights decorated many of the wooden stands as early-evening dusk settled in.

Dane stopped by a large stand in front of Phillips General Store. There were a few women there, carefully examining pieces of pottery. One of the women said to the other, "Maria's work keeps getting better and better. I have about five pieces of it now."

Certainly there was more than one Maria in the town of Red Bluff....

But then Dane saw her. She was on the other side of the stand, making change for a lady who was taking a bag from her. When Dane looked at Maria, the word that came into his mind was *alive*. There was a passion in her that characterized the way she talked, the way she walked, the way she dressed.

After Maria finished with her customer, she turned to the woman at the front of the stand. She must have glimpsed him from the corner of her eye. Her gaze met his, then she looked away, concentrating on her customer's purchase.

The woman bought a vase and after Maria gave her change she went to the next stand. It was then Maria gave Dane her attention. "Is there something I can help you with?" she asked politely.

He suspected she was annoyed with him about yesterday. He had no idea what to do about that. He wasn't about to dredge up everything he was trying to bury. He wasn't about to let anyone get even a glimpse of the part of him that had shattered like a broken mirror after the accident. Picking up a pot striated with blue and green, he peered at the bottom. There was a stamp there, an M above a Y.

"Did you make these?" He waved his hand over the platters and vases.

"It's a pastime," she explained, still being very formal.

"Where do you work?"

"I have a workshop at my parents' ranch."

"And the general store sells them?"

"The general store and a shop in Albuquerque. That's where I was going yesterday afternoon."

He could see Maria had brought up yesterday on purpose. She was definitely a straightforward, let's-confront-the-issues kind of person, and he wasn't used to that. Silence descended between them along with the dusk until a woman with curly red hair who looked to be in her forties came breezing over.

"I'll take over now, honey," she said, patting Maria's arm. Then the redhead looked Dane up and down. "As soon as you tell me who this handsome stranger is," she added.

Maria's cheeks grew a bit rosier as she introduced Dane to Clara Harrihan, the dispatcher at the sheriff's office.

"My sister's husband owns the general store," Clara told him. "So I signed on to help out today. I heard you saved Rod Coolridge's life on Friday. Everybody in town can't wait to meet you now."

"Word spreads fast here," Maria said with a rueful expression.

"One of the many advantages of living in Red Bluff. I don't even need a telephone," Clara added with a chuckle. "Why, I remember when you flew off to Africa to see Tony. The whole town buzzed, and bets were three-to-one you'd be back in a week. And you were."

Now Maria's face was flushed. "I guess that just shows the town knew my marriage was over before I did." She patted the money bag on the makeshift counter behind the merchandise. "I just got change, so you should be all set until it's time to close up."

Clara's gaze fell on Dane again. "Did you have any of our famous Red Bluff chili yet?"

"Not yet. I'm going to get some now. It was good to meet you."

"You, too. I'll be sure to sign up on your side of the clipboard when I visit the clinic next time." With a teasing smile she added, "It wouldn't hurt to make Virgil a little jealous. You take care now."

When Maria stepped off the curb beside Dane, she took one look at his expression and laughed. "I might lose three-quarters of my women patients to you if they think like Clara."

"She wasn't serious."

"She was *absolutely* serious. Clara and Virgil Harrihan are practically newlyweds, though Virgil's not what you might call…the romantic type. He's a deputy for the sheriff's department, too."

Dane shook his head. "You warn me when Clara comes in. I'll make sure we both consult on her case."

When Maria smiled at him again, the tension between them seemed to have diminished. "Have you eaten?" he asked.

She shook her head. "I didn't have a chance."

"Do you have to be somewhere? We could get something."

She glanced at her watch. "I have about a half hour before I need to pick up Sunny."

"Where is she?"

"Over at the school with Joe. He and some other teenagers are playing with the children while their parents are involved with the stands and events."

Maria wore a skirt again today in a crinkly material that molded to her hips and her legs as she walked. Her blouse was the same material as her skirt. Its round neck and full sleeves were very feminine. As

Dane walked down the street with her, her hair rippled across her back. The urge to touch it was so strong, he stuffed his hand into his pocket.

There were several vendors selling chili, and Maria motioned to the one she considered the best.

"Ernesto wins every year. He and his wife have a restaurant on the east side of town. The Cantina. You might have seen it."

"I ate there last night. But I had a steak instead of trying something more exotic."

"We'll liven up your taste buds," she teased.

Right now he didn't need anything more livened up. Having Maria at his elbow was enough to arouse his libido. A woman had never affected him this way before. He felt disloyal to Ellen just thinking about it.

But a few moments later they were each holding a cup of chili and were dipping their spoons into it. After three spoonfuls Dane felt as if smoke must be puffing out of his ears. He coughed, turned back to the vendor and bought a bottle of water.

After he drank half of it, he arched his brows at Maria, who was trying valiantly to suppress her smile. "You enjoyed that, didn't you?"

Her brown eyes danced with amusement. "We didn't even buy the extra hot."

"Okay. Just to show you I'm a good sport, I'll finish the whole cup. But then we're getting ice cream."

Actually, instead of ice cream they opted for lemon ice and found a bench on the periphery of the festivities around the square. The music was pleasant, and several couples danced the two-step. The evening air was getting cooler, the blue sky fading into purple, the lights burning brighter. When Dane's jean-clad knee brushed Maria's skirt, she moved away from him.

Shifting toward her slightly, he asked, "How long have you been divorced?"

She took another spoonful of lemon ice, and the wetness of it glistened on her lips. "Since before Sunny was born."

Surprised, he found himself asking, "Did your husband know you were pregnant?"

After a long moment Maria answered, "By the time I found out I was pregnant and told him, he didn't want *my* child." There was a wealth of hurt in her voice.

"Then he must have been a fool."

Her eyes darted a quick look at him before she returned her attention to her lemon ice. "Thank you for saying that. The truth is, I was as much to blame as he was. When I woke up and wanted to put our marriage back together, he didn't."

"Why?" Dane asked, knowing he had no right to know.

"He'd moved on."

"Even so..."

She shook her head. "By then there was too much hurt between us. And I was so disappointed.... He was a doctor," she explained in a lower voice. "I can't believe he thought I could terminate my pregnancy. That's something I could never do no matter what the circumstances. The fact he suggested it meant he didn't know me at all."

The passion Dane saw in Maria was evident in her words. "You're the type of woman who can only help, not hurt," he said, knowing instinctively it was true.

When she looked up at him, there was surprise in her eyes and maybe even gratitude, but she shook her head. "Don't make me into something I'm not."

For the past two nights Dane had awakened with Maria in his dreams, erotic dreams that were so different from the nightmares since the accident. Now, sitting so close to her, breathing in the scent of her flowery perfume, fighting desire that had too much bite to deny, he reached out and touched a strand of hair that lay against her cheek.

Her gaze never wavered from his. It seemed to ask if he knew what he was doing. It seemed to ask what he wanted.

Damned if he knew.

But her hair was as silky as he imagined it, her cheek as soft. He brushed the back of his knuckles against her skin and felt her tremble. "You have a fire inside of you, Maria, that I've never seen in a woman before."

"I think it's your imagination," she murmured. "You had too much chili."

She gave him a tremulous smile then, and he wanted to kiss her so badly, he was aroused just thinking about it.

When he leaned a little closer to her, she whispered, "People will talk."

He remembered what Clara Harrihan had said about word traveling fast in Red Bluff. He wondered about Maria's family and friends, his position here and the future he was trying to find.

As guitars played in the background, and the scent of chili and tacos and French fries drifted on the air, he asked, "What will they say?"

"They'll say I've been without a man too long, that

you're taking advantage of whatever you can get, that I'm setting a bad example for my daughter."

She wasn't moving away, and that told him she was as attracted to him as he was to her. But her words put a boundary between them that he knew he had to honor. Not only for her sake, but for his. He'd had enough trouble living with himself since the accident. He wouldn't compound his guilt by hurting this woman, too.

He dropped his hand to his thigh. Tearing his gaze from hers was more difficult.

Picking up the dessert he'd placed on the bench next to him, he concentrated on finishing it, paid absolute attention to the cold ice melting in his mouth and tried to put out a fire that had seemed to invade his whole body when he'd touched her. The music filled up the silence until Wyatt Baumgardner came over to them, a broad smile on his face. Instead of his deputy's uniform, he was wearing jeans and a Stetson and a Western-cut shirt.

"Hi, Doc," he said to Dane. "Rod's around here somewhere. He wants to thank you again for saving his life."

"It's just part of the job," Dane said.

Wyatt tipped his hat to Maria. "I thought you might like to do the Texas two-step with me. What do you say?"

There were more couples dancing now as night fell, and the colorful lights added a carnival atmosphere. Dane realized Wyatt and Maria were probably about the same age, midthirties, and he wondered if they'd been dating.

Maria looked at Dane expectantly, maybe waiting for him to object? Maybe waiting for him to claim the dance himself. But he wasn't about to do that. She was the embodiment of vitality and beauty, and he would like to hold her in his arms. He'd like that and a lot more. But he remembered dancing with Ellen, remembered their lives together. He knew what caring about someone and being responsible for them meant, and all of it was simply too painful to contemplate.

So he just nodded toward the other couples. "Go ahead and have some fun."

Maria's eyes flashed almost with defiance then, and she said to Wyatt, "I'd love to dance."

Rising to her feet, she set the lemon ice cup on the bench and took the hand Wyatt offered. The deputy led her to the space under the colorful lights, and she smiled up at him as he took her in his arms and guided her.

But she danced automatically. After a few moments she glanced over Wyatt's shoulder to the bench. Dane was watching, and she couldn't imagine what he was thinking. He'd been ready to kiss her, and she'd been ready to let him. That was insane, especially in this crowd of people.

She could hear her mother's voice now. *He's an Anglo, Maria.* She could hear her father's voice, too. *You've got to think of Sunny.* And even the little voice inside her head was loud and clear. *Don't do anything foolish. Don't get hurt again. Don't set foot in territory that's too dangerous to explore.*

Yet she realized as she danced with Wyatt, that her heart didn't race, her pulse didn't pound, her skin didn't tingle. When Dane had touched her, her whole universe had spun faster and her breathing had become shallow.

What was it about Dane Cameron that intrigued her so?

Wyatt spun her around, and she followed his intricate steps easily. When she again faced the bench where she had been sitting with Dane, she saw he was gone.

Chapter Three

Dane stood at the counter in the exam room and scanned the notes Maria had taken on one of her patients. It was odd how easily he had fitted into the routine at the clinic. This was his fourth day, and he felt as if he'd been practicing here forever. He glanced at Virgil Harrihan. During the man's last visit to the clinic on Monday, Maria had given him a prescription for heartburn.

"It's just not working, Doc," his patient said for the second time.

The burly deputy was Clara's husband and was apparently one of those patients who wanted an instant fix. "It's only been a few days, Mr. Harrihan."

"It's Virgil, Doc, and I know that chili on Sunday could have kicked it off. But I've been having trouble for a while now."

"And you told Dr. Youngbear that?"

"Well, not exactly. I told her it started after I ate the chili. I didn't want her giving me that song and dance about losing weight. She did that last year when I had my physical, and Clara cooked tasteless food for a month.''

Dane's lips twitched, but he suppressed a smile. ''Good food is the key to good health,'' he said, the way a doctor should.

''Yeah, but what fun is it having good health if you can't enjoy yourself along the way?''

Dane had examined Virgil thoroughly and hadn't found anything out of the ordinary. Still... ''I noticed in your records that your father died of a heart attack.''

''Yep. Keeled right over when he was waxing the car one day. He was only fifty-eight.''

Dane paged through Virgil's chart, looking for any bloodwork he might have had done recently. He could find none.

''Clara tells me you're from New York,'' Virgil said.

''Actually, I'm from Connecticut.''

''Went to one of those fancy medical schools, I imagine,'' Virgil prompted.

''I don't know if you'd call it fancy, but they had high standards.''

Virgil's ruddy face grew a little redder. ''So why'd you come here?'' he pushed on, determined to find out what he wanted to know.

Dane closed Virgil's chart. ''I needed a change.''

''I see your hand's kinda stiff. That have anything to do with it?''

If most people noticed, they didn't say anything. But apparently Virgil said exactly what he wanted to, when he wanted to. ''I was a pediatric cardiologist.

Without fine motor skills, I couldn't perform surgery any longer.''

Virgil's brows arched. "Woo-eee. How did it happen?''

"I was in an accident." That was going to be the end of this conversation. "I'm going to order blood-work for you. You can get it done at the hospital tomorrow morning, but you can't have anything to eat or drink except water for twelve hours before.''

"You think this is more than heartburn?''

"I just want to check out a few things. Keep taking the medication Dr. Youngbear prescribed.''

"What do you think of her?" Virgil asked.

The change of subject was unexpected. "I've only worked with her a few days, but...''

"She's a good doctor. I don't mean that.''

"Just what *do* you mean?" Dane asked, pinning Virgil with his gaze.

The deputy shrugged. "Clara said the two of you spent some time together at the cook-off. Maria's a pretty lady. I thought maybe something more was cooking than chili.''

Dane didn't know if he was more annoyed by Virgil's assessment or entertained by it. The thing was—there'd been a strain between him and Maria since Sunday. He'd left without a word to her while she was dancing with Wyatt, and that had obviously upset her. When he'd come into the clinic on Monday morning, she'd been terrifically polite and hadn't gone much beyond civil since then.

It had irritated him to see her dancing with the deputy, yet he hadn't wanted to cut in, because he'd known holding Maria in his arms would be a particularly bad idea.

Now he was trying to find the most diplomatic way to put Virgil in his place. "Mr. Harrihan—"

"Virgil," the deputy reminded him again.

"Virgil, Dr. Youngbear and I are colleagues. We work here together. Once we work together long enough, we might even become friends."

"So you're saying nothing's going on."

Dane shook his head in frustration. "I'm saying I just arrived in Red Bluff on Friday and haven't even moved into my apartment yet."

"The apartment next to Maria's," Virgil added with a sly look.

Apparently the general population of the town were undercover agents! "That apartment just happened to be vacant. Yes."

Virgil chewed on the inside of his lower lip. "Whatever you say, Doc. Can I get dressed yet? This gown's awful drafty."

After Dane lifted Virgil's chart from the counter, he crossed to the door. "You can get dressed. The receptionist will have the form for your bloodwork with your bill."

As Dane opened the door, Virgil said, "Hey, Doc."

Dane glanced over his shoulder.

"Just wanted to tell you in case no one else has. If you *are* interested in Maria...she hasn't dated anybody since she divorced her husband. It would do her good to have a little fun. You know what I mean?"

Dane didn't know exactly what Virgil meant by that, but he wasn't going to explore it. "Thanks for the tip, Virgil." Then he left the examining room, wondering if all his patients would be curious about his personal life.

At five-thirty Dane was at his desk making notes in his patients' charts when Maria came in, looking as if she were armed for war.

"Why did you question my diagnosis of Virgil Harrihan?" she demanded.

"I didn't question it. I told him to keep taking the medication. But since his father died of a heart attack, I want to make sure there's nothing else going on, either. So I'm checking his cholesterol. Do you have a problem with that?"

Some of the stiffness went out of her shoulders. Finally she responded, "No. In fact I suggested it when he had his physical, but he didn't want to be bothered."

"Then there's nothing to get defensive about," Dane decided, his gaze steady on hers.

Instead of averting her gaze as she had since Monday, she kept eye contact. "I suppose not."

The silence between them stretched until he broke it. "Maybe we should clear the air."

"About?"

"About Sunday night."

Her cheeks flushed slightly. "There's nothing to clear."

He kept holding her eyes with his until she said in a rush, "You left without even saying good night!" The words came out as if they'd been pent-up since Sunday.

"You were occupied."

"I danced one dance with Wyatt, and then you were gone."

He shouldn't have started this. Maria's honesty disconcerted him. What would happen if he was as honest with her? "Dancing with you would have been a mistake."

"Why?"

"Because I would have felt disloyal to my wife."

Maria seemed to absorb that. "How long ago did she die?"

"It'll be two years in December."

Instead of commenting on that, which he thought she might, or ask him questions he didn't want to answer, she instead responded, "We didn't have to dance."

Rising from his chair, he remembered the feel of her hair, the brush of his fingers against her skin. "You're a beautiful woman, Maria, but I'm trying to pull a new life together, and I don't need a distraction."

"What do you need?" she asked quite seriously.

Need suddenly took on new meaning as he gazed into her deep-brown eyes, thought about tasting her lips, imagined holding her in his arms. "Damned if I know," he muttered. "But I need simple, not complicated. I'll be moving into the apartment tonight."

"You found furniture over the weekend?"

"I bought a few things. But it won't be delivered until the end of next week. So I'll be sleeping on the floor in a bedroll."

"That beats a motel bed?" she asked with an amused smile.

"Yeah, it does, because the apartment will be my own place, and the sooner I get settled in, the sooner I'm starting my life here."

Again she looked at him with eyes that seemed to see too much. "What kind of life are you looking for, Dane?"

"A peaceful one." He hadn't known peace since before the accident, and it was what he craved most.

"I hope you find it," she said quietly, and then she left the office as quickly and as silently as she'd entered it.

Crossing to the doorway, Dane watched her ponytail sway across her back as she walked. Maria Youngbear was one unique lady, and somehow he had to banish the idea of getting to know her better...he had to banish the idea of holding her in his arms.

Maria heard movement in the apartment next door around 8:00 p.m. She was torn between wanting to welcome Dane to the building and needing to stay away from his penetrating blue gaze. When he'd touched her on Sunday, she'd felt as if her world was going to explode, or worse yet, the world as she knew it would topple over. That had happened to her before—when Tony had decided to go to Africa without her, when she'd flown over there and found he was involved with someone else, when she'd learned she was pregnant. All of those things had been out of her control. But whatever happened between her and Dane now was within her control.

She'd been amazed by her disappointment and pique when she'd found he'd left the square Sunday evening, and it had carried over into her dealings with him since then. That's why she'd been so defensive about Virgil. That and the fact that her qualifications as a woman doctor had been questioned more than once. She'd thought she'd gotten used to it. She knew it went with the territory. But coming from Dane...

Except Dane wasn't questioning it...he was just expanding it.

It was almost nine after Maria had tucked Sunny in for the night. Then restless, she went out on her terrace.

"Interested in a slice of pizza?" a deep male voice asked.

When she turned, the light from inside Dane's apartment cast a shimmering glow onto his terrace. He'd apparently bought two lawn chairs and a small white table. On the table was a cardboard box with a large pizza.

She crossed to his terrace. "Does it feel like home yet?"

"I'm working on it." He waved inside. "I have clothes in the closet and my bedroll set up. I stopped and bought these chairs on the way home, and I can take them in or out. It'll do until the store delivers the furniture."

The dark night was filled with stars, and an almost-full moon enveloped them in intimacy. Maria knew she should run inside and lock her door. But she'd never been a coward, and she had to figure out why Dane intrigued her so. Maybe then the attraction would go away.

He was holding a can of soda loosely in his hand, and he nodded to the pizza again. "Did you have supper?"

"Actually, I didn't. Mom wanted me to stay there and eat, but some nights I just like to get home."

"And be who you are without your family?"

"Something like that. I love them all dearly, but they'd take over my life if I let them. And maybe even run it better than I do,'' she added with a smile. ''But then it wouldn't be mine.''

He slipped a slice of pizza onto a napkin and held it out to her.

''Do you mind if we sit on my terrace? That way I can hear if Sunny calls me.''

''No problem,'' he said with a grin. ''Your chairs look a heck of a lot more comfortable than mine.''

Her patio chairs had frames and cushions and a glass table to go with them. ''I bought for permanence. I think you were just trying for mobility.''

He laughed, a deep rich sound that seemed to fill her as well as the night. Once they were settled on her patio, she said, ''I have a bottle of sparkling cider if you want to toast your moving in.''

''I guess that *is* a good reason to celebrate.''

She went inside, found the bottle in the refrigerator and plucked two stemmed goblets out of a cupboard. When she returned to the terrace, she handed him the bottle.

After he popped the top, he poured the bubbly liquid into the two stemmed glasses. ''Nice crystal.''

''They were a wedding present. They were so pretty I decided that if I tossed them out after my divorce I'd only be spiting myself.''

He studied her for a few long moments. ''How did you learn to be so honest?''

''Hmm. Do you mean honest or blunt?''

His smile eased the lines around his eyes and made him look much younger. ''Sometimes they go together.''

''I guess it comes from having brothers and sisters and parents who don't let me hide from what I'm feeling. That's because *they* don't. They're very...vocal. What about you? Do you have brothers or sisters?"

After taking a sip of the liquid, he shook his head. "Nope. My parents divorced when I was a kid."

"Where are they now?" Maria asked, eager to know more about him.

"My mother's in New York. She's the chief financial officer for a computer company. My dad's in Wisconsin. He teaches history at a university there."

"That's a lot to live up to."

"Tell me about it."

As they ate pizza, drank cider and talked about experiences in med school, the night became cooler.

Maria shivered and Dane noticed. "I still can't get used to how cool the nights are, no matter how hot the day's been."

"One of the perks of living in the desert," she said with a smile, and then shivered again. "I really should be going in. I have rounds at the hospital tomorrow morning before appointments."

When she stood, so did Dane. She'd always thought herself tall at five-six, but he was a good six inches taller than she was. At forty, he couldn't be any leaner or trimmer, and she could see his muscled strength in his upper arms.

She didn't feel she could go inside without mentioning what had happened today. "I'm sorry I was so defensive about Virgil."

"You thought I was questioning your judgment."

She nodded. "I should have spoken to you before I assumed that you were."

He was gazing down at her with such intensity she almost backed away. Almost.

"What?" she asked a bit breathlessly.

"If I had stayed Sunday night, if I'd asked you to dance with me, I would have kissed you."

She swallowed hard, then managed, "But you didn't stay."

"No, and I've what-iffed about it since then. And now here we are—" He slid his hand under her hair, and she stood mesmerized, afraid to move, afraid to breathe, afraid to blink.

"Yes, here we are," she agreed in a murmur, anticipating Dane's kiss, hoping for it, curious about it.

He nudged her toward him slowly as he bent his head, giving her plenty of time to pull back, giving her plenty of time to turn away and run into her apartment. Whatever Maria was expecting, it wasn't the fierce possession of Dane's mouth on hers. He caught her totally by surprise. No sooner had his hot, firm lips branded hers, than his tongue skimmed her lower lip and advanced inside.

When he groaned, Maria felt as if the night had grown darker and deeper and mysterious with desire she didn't understand. In moments she was trembling, and she wasn't sure if it was from passion or fear at what this kiss could mean. The way he claimed her told her his hunger and need were deep. The problem was he sought an answering hunger and need inside of her. It rose up to meet his until her arms went around his neck, until her hands delved into his hair.

What was this fire that she hadn't known existed until Dane's lips had touched hers?

Had she simply forgotten what it was like to be kissed by a man? Is that why she wanted to touch his skin, feel his hands on her, meet every thrust of his tongue with a receptive stroke of her own? Or was something else going on that had to do with who he was or who she was? Something had clicked between them when they'd laid eyes on each other.

She'd been so careful with Tony, making sure he was the right one for her. Respecting her upbringing, they'd gone slowly, become friends and, according to Cheyenne tradition, hadn't slept together until their wedding. Tony had always been gentle and kind, and maybe she'd never really known what passion was.

Dane's desire seemed so much more real, so much more alive, so much more dangerous than anything she'd ever felt from Tony.

Abruptly Dane tore his mouth from hers. When she saw his expression, she pulled her arms from around his neck and dropped them to her sides.

He was breathing raggedly and didn't look at all happy. "You'd better go inside, Maria."

"Or what?" she asked almost defiantly, wanting him to put into words what had just happened between them.

"Or I might kiss you again and that wouldn't be good for either of us."

"I decide what's good for me," she said with some spirit, not wanting him to make decisions for her.

"You might not *know* what's good for you. I'm not. Believe me. For almost two years, I haven't had a life to speak of. I'm finding my way, and whatever it is, I know it's going to be rocky. I also know I have to do it on my own."

She ached to help him, to ease whatever pain was behind the need in that kiss. "Why?"

He shook his head. "It's nothing I want to think about, let alone talk about."

"Does it have to do with your wife?"

"Let it alone, Maria. If we stick to working together we'll be fine. Anything else and we're asking for trouble.''

He wasn't the only one who had a past to deal with. Thanks to Tony, she didn't know if she'd ever be able to trust any man again. Besides that, Dane represented everything her parents would disapprove of. He was white, city-bred, a Northeastener. New York was practically a planet removed from New Mexico and Maria's roots. He was right. If he kissed her again, they'd be asking for trouble. Still, she had her pride. It was all that had kept her going after Tony had abandoned her.

"It was just a kiss, Dane. Nothing to get all worked up about. We'll forget it and go on as if it never happened.'' Then she motioned toward the pizza box. "Thanks for sharing supper with me. After you get moved in, I'll return the favor. I'll see you at the clinic tomorrow.''

And then, before she *did* remember his kiss, she opened the sliding door and went into her apartment, already knowing she'd never forget the way she'd felt in his arms.

Late on Friday afternoon Maria received a call about Virgil's bloodwork. When she caught sight of Dane as he emerged from one of the examining rooms, she knew she had to discuss the results with him.

Forget the kiss. Concentrate on work, she told herself for the umpteenth time since last night.

But whenever she saw Dane, she remembered his taste and touch, and forgetting that kiss seemed almost as difficult as forgetting Sunny's name. Time would do it if willpower couldn't, she decided, as she hurried down the hall and caught Dane before he went in to see his next patient.

When he looked down at her with those blue, blue eyes, she knew neither time nor willpower was going to work. "I got a call on Virgil's bloodwork," she said.

"What did it show?" he asked with the same neutrality that had been evident in all of their dealings with each other since last night.

"He's a prime candidate for a heart attack." She handed the paper to him on which she'd taken notes. "I'm glad you suggested the screening. If we get him on the right path, he can get this under control now."

"That's if he'll cooperate," Dane said with a wry grimace.

"If I get Clara on my side, he'll cooperate."

Dane smiled at that. "Do you want to set up an appointment with him or should I?"

"We'll leave that up to him. I'll have Betsy call him and insist on an appointment, giving him his choice."

Just then the receptionist stepped out of her office and waved to Maria. "Maria, it's your mom. She's in the waiting room with Sunny. Sunny has a temperature of 102."

Fear gripped Maria's heart as it always did when Sunny got sick. Even though she was a doctor, where her own daughter was concerned she relied on prayer as much as her skills.

Hurrying into the waiting room, she found her mother rocking Sunny on her lap. The little girl was listless and flushed, and her eyes had that fevered glaze that Maria knew well.

But when she went to her, Sunny raised her little

arms, and Maria gathered her up. "Come on, baby. Let's see what's wrong." Fortunately her next appointment hadn't arrived, and she had time to tend to her daughter immediately.

Once in the examining room, her mother looked on as Maria attempted to make a game of the examination as she often did with children. But Sunny wouldn't even smile for her. She used the ear thermometer and then gave her a thorough examination.

"What is it?" her mother asked.

"It's an ear infection. No wonder she's so miserable."

Just then there was a knock on the door. When she opened it, she found Dane.

"I saw that you only have one more patient. Do you want me to take him?" he asked.

"That would be great if you could. I'm more worried about tonight, though."

"What's tonight?" Dane asked.

"Mommee," Sunny called to her from the table and held her arms out for her to pick her up.

Maria went to her daughter and scooped her up. "It's okay, baby. Once I get some medicine into you, you'll feel a little bit better." She turned back to Dane who had nodded to her mother with a smile. "I have a workshop tonight at the high school. It's for young mothers—basics about nutrition for themselves and their babies, what to look for in childhood diseases, inoculation schedules. Do you think you could cover it for me?"

Sunny had snuggled into Maria's shoulder and wrapped her arms around her neck. Maria could feel the unusual heat coming from her little body and she rocked her instinctively.

"You can't postpone this?" Dane asked.

"It's so hard to get some of these girls to commit to anything. Several of them are unwed mothers. They signed contracts with me, and this is the first of three workshops they're going to attend." One look at Dane's face told her he really didn't want to do this. She wondered if he had plans tonight. A date maybe?

Maria's mother said, "I can watch Sunny tonight as we planned."

But Sunny mumbled, "Mommee rock?" and Maria knew she couldn't leave Sunny when she was feeling like this. Her eyes met Dane's again. "I have complete notes of everything I was going to cover. All you have to do is read them if you want and then just let the girls ask questions."

After another few moments of deliberation, he agreed. "All right. It's at the high school, you said?"

"Yes, in the home ec classroom. The principal will be there to open it up for you. Let me know how it goes afterward, okay? There are two girls I'm particularly worried about. Sherry and Tessa. They don't have much in the way of support at home."

"I'll make sure the two of them particularly understand everything," he assured her.

Then he studied Sunny and asked, "A virus?"

"An ear infection."

He nodded. "Good to see you again," he said to Maria's mother, then he stepped out into the hall. "Just take care of Sunny. I'll handle anything that turns up here. I'll also tell the service I'll be on call tonight."

"I know this is an imposition—"

But he brushed her words away with the wave of his hand and went to take care of her patient.

* * *

In the course of tending to two end-of-the-day patients who were walk-ins, time slipped by, and Dane went to the Cantina for supper, then directly to the high school. Maria had left detailed notes with the receptionist along with the roster of girls who were supposed to be at the workshop. This wasn't his cup of tea. Besides that, anything to do with mothers and children seemed to twist his heart until it hurt too much to think clearly. But Maria's notes were straightforward and he'd stick to the topics—nutrition, inoculation, child development.

It would be relatively painless, he told himself.

And he believed that until he stepped into the home economics suite of rooms. Chattering and laughter and a few wails sailed toward him from the open door. When he went inside, he realized that these young mothers weren't alone. They'd brought their children with them. There were infants and toddlers and two kids who seemed to be about four. He wanted to step right out of those rooms and close the door.

But then he looked at the young women who had quieted when he entered, and he knew there was no way out of this. He had to just dive right in and somehow reach the shore.

It wasn't so bad as everyone introduced themselves. It wasn't even so bad as he lectured above the noise of the kids playing with the toys in the home ec room, running across the back with the ball or sitting on their moms' laps. But each time he made eye contact with a mother and child the pain in his heart grew and grew, until he felt the hole there was getting bigger and soon he wouldn't have a heart left.

After his lecture he fielded their questions as succinctly as he could. But several of the young mothers needed sounding boards, and he found himself listening to their stories. Sherry told him that her father wanted to kick her out because he needed his sleep at night and her baby kept him awake. There were tears in Tessa's eyes as she told him her boyfriend didn't want anything to do with their son, but he still wanted to have sex with her. He was amazed at the young women's bluntness.

But as he was listening to Michelle like a father confessor, two toddlers played ring-around-a-rosy around his legs, fell down at his feet and laughed up at him.

Every time Dane had looked at Sunny, he'd felt this pain. Every time he thought about children, he felt this pain. He remembered Keith's shining blue eyes, his ready smile, his glee when he'd taken his first step. Dane remembered all of it so well it still seemed real. He'd avoided children since the accident because it was easier, because it hurt less, because he felt less guilty about what had happened to his wife and son. But now with these young mothers and kids all around him, he couldn't push it to the back burner. He couldn't ignore it. He couldn't tell himself it was better.

By the time he left the high school, he felt wrung out and caught in a squall of pain and regret that was too difficult to deal with. It became anger—anger at Maria because she'd put him in this position. She could have canceled the damn workshop. She could have postponed it.

Worse yet, he was angry at himself that he'd agreed to do it.

That fiery kiss with Maria had been a warning flag

that he'd been numb for too long. Why had he done the chivalrous thing and covered for her? Being selfish wasn't always being cruel. Being selfish was sometimes necessary.

As he drove back to his apartment, too many feelings were rushing through him to count. He kept seeing his wife's face, heard her cry out again as he always did in his nightmares.

By the time he'd parked near his apartment, sweat had beaded on his brow and he was still filled with bitterness and aching and frustration. He didn't know what to do about any of it. He went up the stairs, and instead of letting Maria know he was back, he changed into his running gear and then went for a jog. He didn't care that the night was black without a moon, he didn't care that he didn't know his way around Red Bluff yet, he didn't care if a car came speeding by and ran him over. He didn't know how long or how far he ran. He just ran, trying to leave all of it behind him. But he couldn't. It was on his shoulders and in his heart.

Dripping with sweat, exhausted, he finally returned to his apartment, went to his refrigerator for a can of beer and then stepped out to his terrace. Sucking in great lungfuls of air, he tried to sweep it all out of his head. But he couldn't, and after a few gulps of beer, he put the can down on the small table remembering he was on call.

When he set the can on the table, it fell over, knocking loudly, and the beer spilled on the flagstone.

He swore, and his voice carried in the night.

When he heard Maria's screen door open, he didn't want to see her. He didn't want anything to do with her or Sunny and the pain that watching them caused him.

She was surprised when she spotted him in his running gear. "Did you give the workshop?" she asked with worried concern.

Maria was wearing white knit shorts and a sleeveless pink top. She was in her bare feet. Her hair was loose around her shoulders, and in spite of everything else he was feeling, he was so blasted attracted to her he wanted to swear again.

"I did your damn workshop. The next time you can't keep a commitment, you can find someone else to cover for you." The bitterness edging each of his words had an undesired effect. She moved closer to him instead of running away.

"What is it, Dane? What happened?"

After mowing his hand through his hair, he motioned to her apartment. "Go back to your place, Maria. Take care of your daughter and leave me the hell alone."

Chapter Four

Dane knew his harsh words would have sent most women running. But then, Maria wasn't most women.

She stood there studying him in silence for a few moments until she asked again, "What happened?"

"You neglected to tell me the mothers would be bringing their children with them."

"Most of them have enough trouble getting day care so they can work, let alone finding baby-sitters that they have to pay at night," she returned matter-of-factly.

"I don't want a discourse on young mothers, Maria. I heard firsthand how tough it is for them. They must have thought I was some sort of father figure they could unload on while the kids were running around—"

Her gaze was as pointed as her words. "It seems kind of odd that you don't like children when you were a pediatric cardiologist."

They had come to the brink of this discussion once

before. "Damn it, Maria, I don't want to get into this!"

"I think you're already in it, and so am I. If you have a problem with kids—"

"I *don't* have a problem with kids. Not the way you mean anyway. It's just seeing them with their mothers... It brought back everything I came to Red Bluff to forget. Everything I'll always remember."

Now she came a few steps closer to him. "Tell me."

There were no sounds in the night until, frustrated with her persistence, he agreed. "All right! I had a wife and a child. And I had a life. But now I don't and it was all my fault."

"What was all your fault?"

Maria's soft question made him hurt more, and the concern in her eyes finally encouraged him to let go of everything that had been building inside for so long.

"It was early December," he began, his voice low. "We were driving to a ski resort in Vermont. I'm still not exactly sure what happened. Snow had been falling for most of the trip. But I'm used to four-wheel drive and the slick roads in New England."

He looked up at the sky, searching for a moon, searching for a light he hadn't been able to find ever since the accident.

When Maria laid her hand on his shoulder, it was cool against his hot skin, and her touch triggered the rest of the nightmare.

"The accident happened so fast it's still a blur. They told me there was nothing I could have done, but I don't believe it. I was an experienced driver."

"You skidded?" she guessed, pressing him on.

''There was a curve. The truck was coming toward us much too fast. His bright beams blinded me. When he skidded on a patch of ice, he swerved into my lane. We were pushed over the embankment, rolled and smashed into trees. Then the truck plowed into us. I heard Ellen's cries. I tried to reach out to her. I tried to reach back to Keith. But then I lost consciousness.''

He thought he felt Maria's fingers tremble on his shoulder but he couldn't tell for sure. ''I was in a coma for two days. When I awakened, the doctor told me my wife and son were dead. I hadn't begun to wrap my mind around that when I saw the cast on my wrist and hand.''

''Oh, Dane.'' His name on her lips was a sigh and a prayer, filled with a deep sadness that told him she might understand. That brought his gaze from the sky to her. When he looked into her deep-brown eyes, he felt his throat tighten.

Looking away again, far into the desert, he went on. ''There was another surgery on my hand after that and another six weeks after that until I realized my career as a pediatric cardiologist was over, at least in the operating room. They told me with physical therapy, I *might* be able to operate again. But I still couldn't absorb it all. So I took a leave of absence for three months.''

''What did you do?''

''I holed up in our house in Connecticut, I drank, I swore and I cursed fate. Finally I realized life as I'd known it was over. So I sold the house and everything in it and went back to New York to our apartment. My apartment. I didn't see how physical therapy would ever get my hand working again with the fine coordination I need in the operating room, so I dismissed the idea. I became a consulting cardiologist. But after a year of that..."

He shook his head. "I'd had enough—enough of everything about my old life. About that time I saw the notice in the newsletter about the position in Red Bluff, and for the first time since waking up in the hospital, something almost excited me. A general practice someplace where doctors were needed. It just seemed to call to me, so I sent you my résumé."

Taking a deep breath, he faced her again. "I didn't expect moving here to change what happened in the past. I'd hoped it would give me motivation to find a future. But then tonight everything just blew up in my face. The past is never going to go away. I'm never going to stop grieving or missing my wife and child or feeling guilty about what happened."

"I'm so sorry about your wife and child."

There were tears in Maria's eyes, and he couldn't stand that. "I don't want your pity, Maria."

"What do you want?" she asked quietly.

"Right now I think I just need to be left alone."

"Don't give up yet," she said as if she knew what she was talking about. "Grief and loss don't go away, but the intensity does lessen."

"Have you ever lost a spouse or child?"

She kept her gaze locked to his. "I lost a spouse in a different way."

"It's not the same. I'm responsible, Maria."

"I was responsible, too."

He just shook his head, not seeing it at all. Divorce and death were totally different.

"Nothing is forever, Dane. Not even the deep pain

you're in now. It'll pass. Everything does. Not completely, but enough so that you can go on.''

"Where did you get those words of wisdom?" he asked almost angrily.

"My mother. And she's a wise woman. Is there anything I can do?"

Dane knew there was something they both could do. It might make him forget, maybe even for a few moments. He wanted to reach out and touch Maria, but he knew that wouldn't be good for either of them. Not now. Not tonight.

"Go back inside, Maria. I'll ride this out. I always do."

"You don't have to do it alone," she said so sincerely that he could almost believe her.

"No one can help with this. No one can make it go away. No one can make it better."

"Have you given anyone the chance?"

"That's as much a risk as believing in dreams."

"Dane…"

"Go inside, Maria," he said again.

Though she looked torn, she seemed to realize she couldn't help him right now. Maybe not ever. "All right. But I'm not going to pretend tonight didn't happen. You shouldn't, either." Then she crossed to her terrace and went inside.

Dane was filled with regret and longing and a need to go after her that he didn't understand. But it was a need he was going to deny. The last thing he wanted in his life right now was a woman. He'd concentrate on his practice here…and that would be enough.

On Monday morning Dane arrived at the clinic before Maria, still trying to push Friday night into the past with everything else he didn't want to remember. He'd spent the weekend away from his apartment... away from Maria. He was learning his way around Albuquerque and the surrounding area. Sight-seeing certainly wasn't a cure-all, but it was a distraction that absorbed some of his restlessness and the longing to spend more time in Maria's company.

Because writing with his left hand was painstakingly slow, Dane had decided to use tapes to keep notes on each of his patients. He played the tape and then carefully transcribed his observations onto his patients' charts. He'd been working for a half hour when Maria appeared in the doorway, a mug of coffee in each hand.

"Betsy got it going," she explained as she came in and set a mug on his desk.

As his gaze met and held hers, he remembered everything that had passed between them Friday night. "How's Sunny?" he asked.

"Practically as good as new."

Picking up the mug of coffee, he murmured "thanks," not intending to discuss anything else. He should have known it wouldn't be that easy.

Maria sat on the corner of her desk and stared at him over the rim of her mug.

"What?" he asked.

"You could ask for help with patient notes."

"You have enough to do."

"We could look over the budget and see if there's any money for a transcriber. If we had the machine, Betsy might be willing to put in a few hours of overtime."

He thought about it. "If I get backed up, we can consider it."

"There *is* another option," she said matter-of-factly.

Seeing that she had something on her mind, and she wasn't going to leave until they discussed it, he laid down his pen and sat back in his chair. "And what is that?"

"You could let me examine your hand. If I think physical therapy would help, we could get you started on it. You might have full use back before you know it."

"Maybe I don't deserve full use back. Maybe this is retribution for being careless with the people I loved most, for taking them for granted."

Maria's eyes flashed with disagreement. "And maybe this has nothing to do with retribution at all. Maybe you were simply unfortunate enough to be in an accident, on the wrong road at the wrong time. And now you have to make the best of everything you have left."

After a prolonged silence Dane asked her, "Do you believe in God?"

"I believe in someone greater than I am who knows and understands a lot more than I do."

"Do you follow Cheyenne beliefs?"

"My ancestors converted to Catholicism. But there's a lot of wisdom in Cheyenne ways, and my family keeps those alive, as well. Unlike some folk, I don't find contradictions when I combine it all together. But I don't believe God caused your son and wife to die any more than he caused my divorce. We make choices. They lead us in certain directions and then we face the consequences of them."

After studying her for a long time, he tried to think about what had happened in those terms. "I worked more than I saw Ellen and Keith. After the accident, I realized she'd been the parent. I'd been absent more than I was there.''

"A specialty practice is demanding.''

"Yes, it was demanding. But I loved the work, too. I could have lightened my caseload, been more selective about the cases I took. But they *all* seemed important. I wanted to save every child, and I ended up losing mine.''

"The two aren't connected,'' she said firmly.

"Maybe you can see that, but I can't.''

Silence again filled the room until Maria finally broke it. ''Let me examine your hand,'' she requested softly.

She wasn't wearing her lab coat yet. Today she'd donned a collarless blouse patterned in geometric shapes and colors of turquoise, yellow and white. The brightness of it, together with her white jeans, emphasized the rich dark color of her hair and eyes. Already he knew Maria was a persistent woman. If he didn't let her do this now, she'd ask again.

"All right,'' he said, getting to his feet. As he looked down at her, nothing was all right, though. Everything seemed out of sync, including a need for her that should be easy to banish but wasn't.

Suddenly she smiled at him, and the power of that smile almost made him forget his name. But then she beckoned him to follow her, and they went into an examination room. He realized she was going to make this official, that she was going to do a thorough job.

"Sit up there,'' she said, indicating the examination table.

"Maria...'' His impatience brought her head up.

"Are you one of those doctors who's a terrible patient?" she asked with amusement.

"Of course not," he said indignantly.

She laughed. "Good." Then she waited expectantly for him to do as she'd asked.

With a sigh of resignation, he leaned against the table instead.

Shaking her head, she took his hand in hers quickly...before he was ready. He'd needed a few moments to prepare for her skin touching his. But he didn't have them.

Maria took the weight of his hand into hers. His was so much larger, his skin rougher, and the differences between male and female were very evident, even in their hands. She circled her thumb over his palm, and he felt every burning sensation of it. His whole body did. She didn't probe at first, just felt the muscles. But each path of her thumb along a finger, over a ridge, along the side was enough to make him need a cold shower. When she turned his hand over, the scar reminded him why she was doing this. She felt along it, pressing lightly, watching his expression.

"Does that hurt?"

"No." His tone was clipped and when she raised her head and her gaze met his, her cheeks reddened.

"I want to be thorough," she murmured.

She was being thorough all right. Thorough enough to make need and want and desire too intertwined to separate.

Then she had him bend each finger as she studied his hand, keeping her thumb on his wrist.

Finally she said, "I think you know physical therapy can help this. I can't say whether you'll improve enough to be able to do surgery again or not, but you could certainly improve enough to write again, to use your right hand more than you are now. I think you know that, too. So the question is whether you want to or not. Punishing yourself for the accident won't bring your family back.''

Dane knew *that* better than anyone. But he also knew that even weeks of physical therapy might not bring back his fine-motor skills. Maybe he wasn't ready to absolve himself of guilt. Maybe he wasn't ready to let go of an injury that was a connection to his wife and son. It was an odd thought and one he hadn't had before, but he realized it might be true. He could see Ellen's face a little less clearly each day now. Keith's childish chatter was becoming a fading echo. But he didn't know how to say any of that to Maria. He didn't know how to explain the gut-wrenching ache that lanced through him whenever he saw her with Sunny.

The erotic wave of sensation her touch evoked was as unsettling as all the rest. Pulling his hand away from hers, he dropped it to his side. ''We have patients to see.''

''But you'll think about physical therapy?'' she asked with more than a doctor's concern in her eyes.

''I don't have time to go running to Albuquerque for rehabilitation.''

''We could start the therapy right here, in the mornings before we see patients. Since we don't have a hospital in Red Bluff, sometimes I get my patients started. I can do that for you.''

''You have all the answers, don't you?'' he asked, almost bitterly. There was something about Maria, faith or confidence, that told him she knew who she was and what she believed. He was envious of that because he didn't know either anymore.

"I don't have answers," she responded quietly. "But I can help you get the use of your fingers back if that's what you want."

He couldn't look into those dark eyes of hers a moment longer without wanting a life filled with more than work, without feeling even more guilty than he did already about what he had and hadn't given Ellen and Keith. "I'll think about it."

Then he left the examination room, flexing his fingers, trying to ease the ache that Maria's touch had begun.

Cleaning her apartment on Saturday afternoon with Sunny "helping," Maria heard a commotion out in the hallway, then she remembered—Dane's furniture was being delivered today.

Since the morning when she'd examined his hand, they hadn't spoken much. She'd crossed some boundary that day into his personal territory, and he had to make the decision whether he was going to let her in or keep her out, whether he was going to heal from what had happened to him or stay mired in it. She knew how hard it was to let go of memories and dreams. She'd had to do that when she returned from Africa...when Tony had suggested she not go through with her pregnancy. Letting go of Tony and the life she'd wanted to share with him was the hardest thing she'd ever had to do. Sunny's birth had accelerated the process.

But Dane...Dane was stuck in a type of limbo where the past was still more real than the future.

Trying to maneuver her attention away from Dane,

she looked across the coffee table at her daughter who was swiping the dust rag over the wood as if she knew exactly how to use it.

Maria smiled. "How about a nap?"

Sunny looked up at her with big, brown eyes and shook her head.

Some days Sunny took a nap and some days she didn't. Maria had learned long ago that it was better to go with the flow rather than fight about it.

Suddenly there was noise outside beyond the terrace, and Maria saw two men carrying a long sofa past her patio.

"Go see," Sunny said with determination as she ran to the screen.

Maria had seen the look in Dane's eyes every time his gaze fell on her daughter, and now she understood why his caring for children caused him pain. So she knew he wouldn't want Sunny getting underfoot. "I don't think so, little one. Why don't we get a snack instead. How about peanut butter crackers and juice?"

Sunny was entranced by the men outside and she didn't answer. Still, Maria knew once her daughter had the peanut butter crackers in her hand, she'd forget about everything else.

In a few moments Maria had prepared Sunny's snack and moved it from the counter to the kitchen table. Yet when she called, her daughter didn't come.

Going into the living room, Maria saw the open screen door onto the terrace and panicked. She rushed to it, calling Sunny's name. She mustn't have latched the door securely enough the last time she used it.

Maria was outside in an instant and breathed a sigh of relief when she saw her daughter standing at

Dane's terrace doors, her nose pressed against the glass.

"Wanna see," she said to her mother as if she'd expected Maria to follow her.

At the same moment Dane saw Sunny standing at his door. He was dressed in navy shorts and a red-and-white-striped polo shirt, looking too handsomely casual for Maria to turn away. He opened the door before Maria could scold Sunny for leaving their apartment without her, before she could prepare for the impact of seeing him outside of the clinic.

When he opened the sliding door, he smiled down at Sunny. "Hi, there."

"Wanna see," she told him, too.

He laughed. "There's not a whole lot to see."

Taking Sunny by her shoulders, Maria started to turn her toward their terrace. "I'm sorry she bothered you. You must be in the middle of trying to get everything in order."

"Actually, the movers just left and I'm trying to decide where to put everything. They brought the sofa in the back because it was easier."

Sunny shrugged away from her mother's hand and ran inside his apartment, going to the new couch and flopping herself on it.

Maria started after her, shaking her head. "There's a snack waiting for you next door."

But Dane caught Maria's elbow. "I could use a little decorating advice. I bought all the pieces but don't know where to put them."

She looked up at him and her breath caught. Was he inviting her into his life? No. That was reading too much into it. Still...his fingers on her arm were branding her, and the current buzzing between them was enough to light up Red Bluff for a week.

As he dropped his hand, she tried to calm her racing pulse. "You bought a lot of furniture," she said as she looked around.

The sofa, chairs and occasional tables sat in the middle of the living room waiting to be placed. Dane had two walls free, and he had to decide where he wanted to put the groupings. There was also a television on an oak stand as well as a set of bookshelves. She liked the colors of the fabric which were mostly in earth tones, except for the forest-green leather recliner that she supposed would be Dane's most-used chair.

After a few moments of deliberation, she suggested, "I think the sofa would be best against the inside wall. I'll help you move it."

For the next hour Dane and Maria pushed furniture, rearranged, laughed and caught each other's gazes for long moments before looking away. Maria's body hummed whenever Dane got within touching distance, and her flushed cheeks were from more than exertion. Sunny had wandered about the apartment, tried out Dane's bedroll that was now dumped on his kitchen floor, stood in awe of the king-size bed in the bedroom and then bounced a few times on it.

Finally, as Maria and Dane were looking over their handiwork, Sunny came running to her mother, looked up at her and said, "Hungee."

Maria checked her watch. It was almost five. "I guess you are. Your snack's still sitting on the counter. Come on, we'll leave Dane in peace to enjoy his new furniture."

"Why don't you stay for supper?" he asked, his

gaze pinning Maria still. "It's the least I can do for your help. I stocked the cupboards and refrigerator this morning. Do you like hot dogs?" he asked Sunny.

She bobbed her head enthusiastically. "Mus-tar'"

He laughed. "I think I remembered mustard. I can try out my new grill. What do you say?"

"Are you sure?" Maria asked.

"I'm positive. Unless you have plans for tonight."

Was he asking her if she had a date? She almost laughed. "No plans," she said lightly.

While Dane grilled the hot dogs, Maria prepared a salad. They also added a bag of tortilla chips from his kitchen and cookies she'd made that morning for Sunny from hers. Dane moved one of Maria's chairs to his patio, and they talked about patients and the area, staying away from any serious subject. While Sunny was eating her hot dog, it slipped from the roll and she managed to smear mustard all over her fingers.

Dane was closer to her and grabbed her plate and hot dog before it fell to the flagstone. "Uh-oh. I think you need some help." Taking his napkin, he tenderly wiped the mustard away from the side of Sunny's mouth and then from her hands.

After he did, Maria saw him take a deep breath, and she wondered if he was remembering another child at another time.

But instead of backing away from Sunny as he'd done before, he popped her hot dog back into its roll and held it for her. "Now try it," he suggested.

Gazing up at him with large, trusting eyes, Sunny took a bite and then smiled at him—one of those smiles that came straight from the angels.

Maria's chest tightened, and she wondered what Dane was thinking and feeling. But other than the nerve working in his jaw, she could tell nothing else from his expression. He was quiet after that, though, and as they finished supper, the atmosphere had changed. After Maria wiped Sunny's face and hands more thoroughly, she found a program on the TV that her daughter could watch while she and Dane cleaned up.

Dane brought in the remains of the salad and the plate of cookies, nodding to his living room. "I think Sunny fell asleep."

Maria transferred one of Dane's new ironstone dishes to the dishwasher. "She still needs naps even though she doesn't want to take them. Maybe I want her to take them so she'll stay my baby longer."

"They grow up much too fast," Dane said in a husky voice.

"How old was Keith?" Maria asked.

Dane's head jerked up at the unexpected question. "He was five."

"Had he started kindergarten?"

"That September."

Maria waited, giving Dane the chance to go on if he wanted to.

"No one ever mentions him to me. Or Ellen."

"That's because they can see your pain when they do."

"And I thought I was hiding it so well," he returned wryly.

"You can't hide that much grief, Dane. And you can't ignore it, either. Friends and family think by not talking about loved ones it helps. But it doesn't.

They're always there...in the space...beside and around you.''

Looking surprised at her insight, he asked, ''How do you know that so well?''

Maria put a few more dishes into the dishwasher. ''I was very close to my grandmother—my mother's mother. I think I felt closer to her than anybody else on this earth. She died when I was fifteen, and I thought that by not thinking about her I'd feel better. Then one weekend I went hiking in the desert to try to come to terms with losing her. It was as if she was all around me, everywhere I turned, smiling at me, putting her hand on my shoulder, trying to show me she was with me and would never leave. Not thinking about her was making the grief worse. So I did the opposite. I tried to remember everything. When I came home, I told my mom conversations Gram and I had had that she'd never known about. We ended up laughing and crying together and somehow feeling her presence even more strongly.''

''Sometimes I feel as if there's a war going on inside me,'' he admitted. ''One part of me's trying to forget. The other part's trying to remember.''

''Both sides will make peace with each other, but you have to let them.''

He came closer to her then, and settled his hands on her shoulders. They were large and warm, and heat from them shot through her whole body. ''I've never talked to anyone about any of this. I never imagined I'd be talking about it now with you.''

She didn't know what this connection was between her and Dane, but it felt more powerful than anything she'd ever felt before. Could it be she simply had never known true attraction?

The pressure on her shoulders increased slightly as Dane slowly bent his head. His blue eyes mesmerized her until she didn't even think about turning away. When his lips met hers, there was expectancy and possession and a demand greater than any she'd felt before from him. Her arms went around his neck as she kissed him back answering his hunger, fulfilling his need. Everything in her world faded into Dane. His passion was alive, sparkling, lighting fires inside of her that burned deeper than any passion she'd ever shared with Tony. Her experience with men was limited. But this keening ache that increased whenever Dane touched or kissed her made her believe it was singular, set apart, extraordinary.

As Dane's tongue breached Maria's lips, she clung to him, laced her fingers into his hair, and held on for the ride. When he nudged her closer to him, she went willingly, her hips meeting his, her breasts pressing into his chest, her breath becoming a sigh of satisfaction.

She wasn't prepared for the explosion when he pushed into her primitively and she felt his arousal, wanting the satisfaction it would give her.

But that wanting stopped her. That wanting made the sensual haze begin to clear. That wanting scared her almost as much as the sensuality of everything that was happening between them. If Dane was letting her into his life, she didn't know how he fitted into hers. Did he want an escape from his past? Did she want something she'd never known? Could she trust a man to stay? Could she trust a man to not change his mind about wanting her?

And what about Sunny?

Right now Dane could hardly stand to be around children.

All of the questions brought a dose of reality that Maria had to face.

She backed away from him, tearing free, still trembling from the desire that had pushed them together and was now tearing her apart. "I'd better go," she said quickly.

"Maria..."

She shook her head. "I don't know what this is between us, Dane. I don't know if it's an escape from reality for you, if it's a dose of excitement for me. But whatever it is, we need to think carefully about it before we get swept into something that's only going to hurt us both."

Dane's blue eyes were stormy now, his broad shoulders tense. "Pleasure can be simply pleasure, Maria. Can't we accept it for what it is?"

"I'm not made like that," she said softly. "I can't imagine being intimate with a man and then saying goodbye in the morning."

"And I'm not ready to consider the possibility of more than that."

He'd put it into words, and those words were a blow to her heart. Her feelings for Dane were growing deeper, but apparently his feelings were at a standstill. They might have even died with his wife.

She could feel the prick of sudden tears, and she blinked them away knowing she was being foolish. She hardly knew Dane, she told herself. There was no reason they couldn't simply be neighbors and colleagues. They didn't have to be more. They *couldn't* be more.

She crossed to his living room then, knowing there was nothing else to say.

But before she could pick up her sleeping daughter, Dane was gathering Sunny into his arms. "I'll carry her over for you."

The sun had begun its descent, and Dane's face was shadowed in the living room. Going ahead of him, she opened the screen to the terrace and stepped outside...maybe stepping out of his life.

Chapter Five

Maria had been ignoring Dane all week, and it was beginning to annoy him. After he'd taken Sunny over to her apartment on Saturday evening, they'd said formal goodbyes. It had seemed fake somehow. Formality didn't belong between them. Yet he knew Maria's polite formality was a barricade against the desire they both felt. He wanted to act on it. She didn't. Neither of them were right. Neither of them were wrong. They were just different.

He'd stopped in his office Friday morning to pick up a blank tape for his recorder when Betsy buzzed him. After he snatched it up, the receptionist said, "It's the high school on line two. They need to talk to either you or Maria."

"I'll take it," he said, absently checking his watch. The waiting room was empty for the moment, and he had an hour till his next patient.

"Dr. Cameron, here. How can I help you?"

"This is Coach Elwin," a deep male voice said

over the phone. "We had a little trouble. The boys were practicing for football and one of them started a scuffle. Joe Eagle fell and hit his head. He says he's fine, but I thought we'd better call someone."

Joe Eagle. Dane wondered if that was Maria's brother. Whether it was or not, a concussion could be serious. "I'll be right there. Just keep him quiet."

Less than ten minutes later the school secretary led Dane into the boys' locker room. The coach was sitting beside Joe on a bench along the stand of lockers. The teenager looked up, and Dane could see it *was* Maria's brother. The boy didn't look happy to see him.

The coach gave Dane a nod and said, "I'll be outside."

Dane put down his bag and took out a penlight along with his stethoscope.

Joe eyed him warily. "I'm fine. I just bumped my head, that's all."

"Are you dizzy?"

Joe shrugged. "Not really."

But Dane wasn't going to let the boy evade him. "Either you are or you aren't, Joe. Don't hide symptoms on this. They could be serious."

"I told you, I'm fine."

"You want to tell me what happened?" Dane asked.

The boy looked as if he was going to say "no" but then everything spilled out. "Trevor called Maria a name. I tried to walk away but then he shoved me between my shoulder blades and called me 'chicken.' I fell and everyone laughed."

While Dane absorbed all of it, he told Joe to breathe a few times and he listened to his chest. When he was finished, he told Joe to look at a spot above his shoulder. Then he shone the penlight into the teenager's eyes. "What are you going to do if something like this happens again?"

After a few moments of silence the teenager asked, "Why should you care?"

Dane noted that both Joe's pupils were mutually reactive. "I don't like to see anyone get hurt."

Joe seemed to think about that.

After a thorough examination, Dane couldn't find anything seriously wrong with Joe. But he knew the boy should be watched closely by his parents for the next day or so, just in case.

Finished with the examination, he spoke to the coach about the incident, then said, "I think I'm going to take Joe home myself. I'd like to talk with his parents. They need to keep an eye on him for the next day or two."

"You being the doc and all, I guess that's okay. I'm glad you came instead of Dr. Youngbear since this seemed to be about her."

"She would have handled it as professionally as I have."

"Oh, I know that. She's a class act. But it would have been awkward."

During the drive to the Eagles' ranch, Dane thought about what the coach had said.

Joe didn't seem inclined to conversation and wore a sullen expression.

Finally Dane asked, "What's wrong? You should be thankful for a private taxi service."

"I didn't want my parents to know what happened."

"You might have a concussion and that could be

dangerous. There are certain things your parents need to watch for.''

There was more silence after that until Dane asked, ''What did Trevor call Maria?''

''You don't want to know,'' Joe mumbled. ''And don't go telling her what happened, either.''

''I don't keep those kinds of secrets, Joe. From what I understand, the coach and half the team heard what was said. You don't think word's going to get around?''

The teenager gave one of those half shrugs that always frustrated adults.

For some reason Dane felt the responsibility for helping Joe think through what had happened. ''If Trevor does try to start something again, you've got to figure out what you're going to do.''

Joe was silent.

Looking for a way to connect with him, maybe because of Maria, maybe not, Dane said, ''It's best to walk away if you can. But when you can't...I know self-defense if you want to learn a few moves.''

Now Joe seemed interested in conversation. ''Where'd you learn self-defense?''

''I grew up in New York City, and I took a few classes.''

''Ever had to use it?'' he asked with eager curiosity.

''Twice—with muggers.''

''You're serious?'' Joe asked as he shifted toward Dane.

''Sure am. It's an everyday thing there.''

''What did you do to them?''

''It's what *they* didn't do to *me*. The first one had a knife and got my wallet. When he went for me, I managed to dodge him. The second time the guy went for my watch and he got a kick in the groin.''

With a sideways glance Dane could see a small smile play on Joe's lips.

Then he added, ''As I said, I don't believe in hurting anybody. But you have a right to defend yourself, and good defense moves can go a long way in getting a bully's respect.''

The Eagle ranch was about fifteen minutes east of Red Bluff. Joe directed him through a few turns onto secondary roads between red bluffs that rose against the blue sky. Finally the sixteen-year-old told him to turn down a gravel lane. Dane's SUV kicked up enough dust to be seen for a mile.

Pulling up to a sprawling, stucco rancher trimmed in chocolate brown, he noticed it had a red-barrel tile roof. The property was well kept, and he could see horses under an overhang in the corral. When he scanned the outbuildings, he wondered which one housed Maria's workshop.

As he and Joe walked up to the front door, the door opened and Maria's mother stood there.

''What's wrong?'' she asked with that intuition that most mothers have.

''I'm fine,'' Joe mumbled. ''Don't let him tell you differently,'' and he brushed past her and went inside.

With a brief explanation, Dane related to Carmella what had happened at school and told her she needed to watch Joe for symptoms of dizziness or nausea or disorientation. If any of those occurred, she should take her son to the hospital in Albuquerque at once.

Carmella looked up at Dane and studied him for a few moments. She was a small woman, a good four inches shorter than her daughter. She wore her hair in a braided corona around her head. Her eyes were as dark as Maria's, and now they seemed to see through him. "Thank you for bringing him home. You didn't have to do that."

Before he could respond, a little whirlwind came running to the door, and he felt his legs gripped with small arms. He looked down, saw Sunny and froze. How many times had Keith run to him like this? But then the memories receded and he focused his attention on Sunny's smiling face that said she was happy to see him.

Stooping over, he picked her up. "And what have you been doing today?"

"Eatin'. Playin' wif clay. You play?"

He laughed. "I'd really like to play in the clay with you, but I've got to get back to where your mommy works. We have a lot of patients to see." Then he put her down.

Carmella had watched the whole interchange with interest. "You didn't have to go to the trouble of bringing Joe home. Please accept my thanks by coming to dinner on Sunday."

"No thanks are necessary—" he began.

"Sure, they are. Besides, we'd like to get to know you better. After all, you work with our daughter."

It seemed Carmella was as plain speaking as Maria was. In other words the Eagles were going to look him over and see just what kind of man Maria had chosen to practice with. It was a challenge.

"All right. That would be great. I'm already tired of my own cooking. What time?"

"Come around noon."

With a nod of assent and a wave to Sunny, he left

the Eagles' ranch, wondering what he was getting himself into, accepting Carmella Eagle's invitation.

When Dane returned to the clinic and checked with Betsy, he found he had ten minutes before his next appointment. Stopping in the office, he found Maria working at her desk.

She leaned back in her chair. "Mom called to tell me what happened. Is Joe really all right?"

"I just left your mother's ranch!"

Maria checked her watch. "Fifteen minutes ago. Mom's a fast talker. Though Joe wouldn't talk about what happened. Do you know?"

"Just something between guys."

She eyed him suspiciously. "If you don't tell me, Joe will. He might not tell Mom, but he'll tell me."

Dane wasn't so sure about that.

When he still remained silent, she tilted her head. "Oh, I see. This had something to do with me?"

Going over to his desk, Dane sat on the corner. "It's better if you leave it alone, Maria."

After an exaggerated sigh, she said, "You're too chivalrous, Dane. I'm sure you've heard that old saying about sticks and stones. I had to accept that one long ago. I'm a woman, Cheyenne, a doctor and divorced."

This gave Dane an opening he'd been waiting for. "Where's Sunny's father now?"

Pushing back her chair, Maria stood and leaned against her desk, facing him. "He's still in Africa."

"When Clara Harrihan made some reference to Africa the day of the chili cook-off, I thought she was kidding."

"No. Tony decided he wanted to expand his horizons. At first he wanted me to go there with him. It *is* a thoroughly unselfish method of serving mankind. But I guess I wasn't unselfish enough. I couldn't handle the idea of leaving my family and everything I was familiar with. I'd missed them terribly throughout college and med school.''

"Tony wasn't from here?''

"Oh, no. He was from Montana. His family had moved around a lot and I think he enjoyed it. He'd never been to New Mexico, and when we took the jobs here at the clinic, he liked it at first. But then I guess he got bored.''

"With Red Bluff...or with marriage?'' Dane asked, sensing an undercurrent beneath Maria's calm words.

"I thought just with Red Bluff. I guess I was naive. I was so angry that he would leave and go to Africa without me, not even considering what I wanted. We didn't even keep in touch. Four months after he left, he served me with divorce papers.''

"You make it sound as if they were a shock.''

"They were. One that woke me up. I still loved him. I had a good friend who made me see that if I wanted to save my marriage I had to do something about it. So I flew to Africa.''

Dane didn't push her for more. Rather, he waited. Seeing the pain in her eyes at the memories, though, he realized she'd moved on but hadn't forgotten.

She continued more slowly now. "At first I thought we were going to have a reunion. Was I naive! After that first night, I found out he was involved with someone over there...seriously involved. He didn't care about our marriage, maybe never had. So I came back home. Six weeks later I found out I was pregnant.''

She shook her head sadly. "But it didn't matter. He didn't want a baby. He thought it would be better if I terminated the pregnancy. He's a doctor, a man who should be safeguarding life. But there he was, telling me he didn't want the responsibility of a child, telling me he didn't want to pay child support. I hadn't even asked."

Dane could hear the deep regret in her voice, the terrible disappointment, the passing of a dream. Even though she hid her pain behind her vitality and bravado, Maria Youngbear had known deep hurt, too.

"Maria," he said, taking her hand between his, looking deep into her eyes. "Your ex-husband is an idiot. I can't imagine having a daughter like Sunny and not wanting to be part of her life."

Maria's eyes were shiny, and he didn't know if it was because of what he'd said or because of what she'd remembered. He'd never wanted to pull her into his arms more. Holding her brought him pleasure, kissing her awakened desire he hadn't felt in years. But doing either right now wouldn't be a good idea. They both had wounds and scars that an affair could make worse. And if he took her into his arms again, that's where they'd be headed.

Releasing her hand, he pushed away from his desk and straightened. "I have at least one patient waiting. I'd better get moving."

She studied him from where she was. "Will Joe be all right?"

"Your mother is watching for signs of a concussion, but I think he's going to be fine."

"Mom told me she invited you for dinner on Sunday."

He crossed to the doorway. "Yes, she did. But I'm not sure it's a good idea."

"If you do come, it'll be a meal to remember," she said, trying to lighten the atmosphere. "My family is a noisy bunch."

The problem was, everything about Maria was memorable. He'd have to think long and hard before he got involved with her family as well as with her.

"So Jase is watching Elizabeth this afternoon?" Maria asked one of her very favorite patients and friend, Allison McGraw. Allison was a nurse-practioner who had worked at the clinic until her baby had been born six weeks ago.

"Watching her?" Allison asked with a smile. "Probably holding her and rocking her and not putting her down for a minute." Allison had dressed after Maria's examination and was now sitting in the chair beside the desk as Maria made notes on her chart.

"She's only six weeks old. He can't have spoiled her rotten yet," Maria teased good-naturedly. She and Jase McGraw, Allison's husband and the sheriff of Red Bluff, had been friends long before Allison had come to town. During Maria's separation from Tony, Jase had been a sounding board. After Allison had arrived in Red Bluff to visit Jase, she'd felt there was more between him and Maria than friendship. But she'd learned otherwise. She and Jase had been married for almost three years now.

"Jase has been wonderful with her," Allison said honestly, brushing her chin-length blond hair behind her ear. "The only thing he minded about her birth was that we can't—'' She stopped and her cheeks flushed.

Maria smiled. Allison was a genuine lady, and discussing her sex life, even with her doctor, was difficult for her.

"Now that won't be an issue, as long as Elizabeth will give you some private time alone," Maria told her. "You've healed nicely and it's up to you whether you're ready or not for sex again."

"Oh, I'm ready," Allison confided, almost shyly.

"Do you need a baby-sitter?" Maria asked. She loved taking care of babies.

"Are you serious?"

"Sure I am."

"Gloria Torres has offered. But she and Frank Nightwalker have been seeing so much of each other lately, she's hardly ever home. And I don't know if Jase would trust just anyone."

"After I make rounds at the hospital on Wednesday, I'll be off the rest of the day," Maria told her friend. "Is Elizabeth taking a bottle yet?"

"I've been using it as a supplement."

"Then why don't you bring her over Wednesday afternoon, and you and Jase can have the rest of the day and evening together."

"That would be wonderful! Are you sure you want to do this?"

"Positive."

"Sunny won't mind?" Allison asked with a laugh.

"She'll help me. With all her cousins, she's used to being around babies. Talk to Jase about it and let me know. Give me a call next week if you want to go ahead with it."

"I'll do that."

Allison picked up her purse that she'd set on the floor by her chair and stood. "How's the new doctor working out?"

"Patients seem to like him," Maria said noncommittally.

"How about you?"

"I like him, too. Maybe too much."

Allison tilted her head. "You're interested in him?"

"Let's just say there's some snap and sizzle between us. But there are a lot more walls, especially on his side, and I don't know if I'm ready to take any giant leaps, either."

"You deserve to be happy, Maria...to have someone special in your life. I know firsthand how frightening that leap can be. I almost lost Jase because I was afraid to try again."

"I don't think he would have let you lose him."

"I don't know. When it comes to matters of the heart, we're all vulnerable. As Jase and I found out, if you don't reach out and take the chance, happiness can slip right through your fingers."

Taking a chance. Life was all about that, it seemed. But even if she was ready to do that, she wasn't sure Dane was. "I know you're right. Maybe it just takes more courage than I've got right now."

"You're the most courageous woman I know, Maria Youngbear. You just need to make up your mind about what you want. Once you do, you'll find it."

Then the two women hugged. With a last smile, Allison opened the door and said, "I'll let you know about next Wednesday."

Maria closed Allison's chart, pleased to see her so

happy, glad to know that she and Jase were soul mates and they were finding a happily-ever-after.

Dane felt out of his element Sunday afternoon as he was introduced to everyone in Maria's family—brothers, sisters, nieces, nephews and even a cousin or two. He'd almost backed out of coming today, but then he'd glimpsed Maria after she'd returned home from church. She'd been wearing a yellow sundress trimmed in green, and her hair had been loose and falling down her back. Sunny was wearing a matching sundress and had looked as adorable as Maria looked beautiful. He decided just watching her for the afternoon was better than trying to sight-see or sit in his apartment with a baseball game on the TV. And there wasn't much chance anything could happen between them here. There were too many chaperones.

Throughout dinner at the large picnic tables on the patio, he listened to the conversations, heard squabbling and sharing, saw hugs and kisses for the little ones. Joe was the only one who watched him warily. Everyone else was friendly.

Maria leaned close to him at the picnic table. "What do you think?" she asked with a smile. "It's sort of like a family reunion every Sunday."

He laughed. "I suppose it's all second nature to you. Seems like a convention to me. Ellen was an only child, and her mom and dad were both deceased. With my dad in Minnesota and my mom too busy to think about getting this much food ready for anyone, I'm not used to family parties."

"Oh, but this isn't a party. This is a weekly occurrence," Maria said with a chuckle and a fond shake of her head.

Dane waved to the food on the table. "Does everyone bring something?" He knew Maria had made enchiladas and stuffed them into the oven as soon as they'd arrived.

"We take turns."

He glanced around again. "This is something special. This *place* is special."

Maria's brown eyes turned all soft and deep, and he could see that she was glad he understood. Her words confirmed it. "This ranch is my home. Sunny and I live at the apartment, but I can't imagine not having this to come to, and I can't imagine everyone not being here when we do. It's why I just couldn't pack up and go to Africa. It's what sustained me through the divorce and having Sunny."

"You're very lucky."

"I know I am, and I count my blessings every day."

How long had it been since Dane counted his blessings?

His arm nestled comfortably against Maria's. There was more than comfort there...and excitement of having his skin touching hers. But it wasn't just sexual. It was pleasant on another level, too. Maria was fast becoming a blessing in his life, and he even looked forward to each new day here.

Carmella's gaze drew Dane's from across the table, and he realized she'd been watching him and Maria. Maybe even listening to their conversation.

Her expression was troubled, yet she said, "Maria tells me you lost a wife and child. I'm sorry about that."

He still wasn't used to Maria and her family speaking plainly, not worrying about convention so much as honesty.

"Mama," Maria said in a warning tone.

But he covered Maria's hand with his. "It's all right. Yes, I did. It'll be two years in December."

"How old was your son?"

"Keith was five. He'd started kindergarten and was growing up so fast. If I didn't watch carefully he grew an inch in a week."

Carmella looked closely at Dane's hand covering Maria's. "Well, I suppose it's time for dessert."

Maria swung her legs over the bench and stood. "I'm going to ask Rita to watch Sunny for a few minutes. Dane, would you like to see my workshop?"

Carmella explained, "We put dessert out on the tables and then keep eating it all afternoon. Have you seen any of Maria's work?"

"Yes, the day of the chili cook-off. But I'd like to see more."

"Come on, then," Maria said with a smile. "I'll talk to Rita, then I'll show you my refuge."

A few minutes later Dane walked beside Maria, the sun beating down on them. The intensity of it matched the heat in his body when he was anywhere near her. Her bare shoulders were captivating. Her hair was glossy, and her brown eyes sparkled.

"I'm sorry about Mama's questions," she said.

Dane thought about dinner and the conversation. "It's all right. I've always thought talking about Keith would make the hurting worse, but actually it was kind of nice remembering."

"Is that true for your wife, too?"

"I don't know. Ellen—" He stopped.

After a few moments Maria asked, "Did you have a good marriage?"

"Do you have a definition for one of those?" Dane returned.

Maria stopped and looked up at him. "Not from my own experience, I guess. After Tony left, I realized everything about our marriage had been kind of shallow. Our backgrounds had brought us together and given us something. We also had our professions in common, and I'd thought that would be enough. But it wasn't. We didn't seem to have life in common. Do you know what I mean?"

He thought about his marriage to Ellen, how little quality time they actually spent together. "I met Ellen on a ski trip, and we loved to ski. We also came from families whose lifestyles were similar. But my work interfered a lot."

"Did she understand?"

"I'm not sure if she understood or if she was just resigned to it. There's a difference."

"I suppose there is."

Maria began walking again then, and the hot, dry air filled his lungs as he thought about the differences between Ellen and Maria and why he was so attracted to Maria.

The adobe structure that Maria led him into was much cooler than outside. There was a fan in the vaulted ceiling.

"This used to be a guest house," Maria explained, waving to the sink and cupboards. "But it was perfect for a workshop."

He could see that. There was a potter's wheel with worktables nearby littered with all kinds of implements—knives and brushes, towels and a basin with water. There were shelves with jars and pots in various stages of completion. One whole section was devoted to paints.

She walked over to the potter's wheel. "You know, working at the wheel would be great therapy for your hand."

Since the day she'd examined his hand, she hadn't alluded to physical therapy again. He'd been too busy to put much more thought into it, and now he let her comment pass.

"So how much time do you actually get to spend here?"

"Most Sundays." She pointed to a miniature table and chairs near the potter's wheel. "Sunny likes to come in here too and play with clay."

"An artist in the making?"

Maria grinned. "She's into abstract art right now. In time we'll see."

After a thorough look around, they went outside again, and Dane caught sight of a few horses that had come near the fence in the pasture. He asked, "Do you mind if I take a look at the horses?"

"No. I didn't think you'd be interested. Do you ride?"

"There was a stable near our home in Connecticut. We used to ride when I had a weekend off." He headed toward a gray Appaloosa who looked friendly. At the sound of their voices, she poked her nose over the fence and looked at him as if she wanted some company. He went toward her with a smile, thinking about how he'd missed riding.

He let the horse smell his fingers and passed his hand down her neck. "She's a beauty."

"She's mine," Maria admitted. "Joe rides her most of the time when I'm too busy."

He looked at the Appaloosa and then at Maria. He could picture her in his mind's eye, the horse's mane and Maria's hair blowing in the wind. "Do you ever ride bareback?" he asked. He had only ever done it once or twice himself and loved the feel of the horse directly under him.

But with his question, Maria's expression changed. She was no longer smiling, and she looked angry. "Like an Indian you mean?"

"That's not at all what I meant." He was annoyed at the way she'd taken his comment. "I can just picture you and the horse riding wild and free. I certainly didn't mean it as an insult."

She was silent for a long time, but she didn't look away from him. "I am Cheyenne, Dane, and you're white. And as much as I'd like to forget, there are stereotypes."

"And you think I see you as a stereotype?"

"I don't know."

His desire for Maria, the need to simply be with her, thrust him into turmoil that he didn't know how to handle. The past was still very much part of him, and before he'd come to Red Bluff, he hadn't even been sure of a future. But Maria had made him feel alive again.

Reaching out, he brushed her hair from her temple and laid his palm against her cheek. "I see you as a beautiful woman." The wind blew Maria's skirt against Dane, ruffled her hair and brought her sweet scent to him.

He was so engrossed in her that when a deep, male

voice asked, "Why don't you two come and have some dessert?" it was a complete surprise.

Dropping his hand from Maria's face, Dane turned and saw her father. Recovering quickly, he said, "You have a wonderful place here, Mr. Eagle."

"It's been in my family for three generations. The land and tradition mean a lot to us, Dr. Cameron."

There was a warning in Thomas Eagle's voice.

"I can see that," Dane assured him, seeing the worried look in the older man's eyes. He was concerned about his daughter and a stranger who didn't belong yet.

And maybe never would.

Chapter Six

Cuddling Elizabeth Anne McGraw close to her, Maria sat on her terrace, enjoying every moment she'd spent with the baby today. She'd put Sunny to bed about half an hour ago and brought Elizabeth's bassinet outside. But she couldn't resist holding the child and remembering the days when Sunny was that small. It was too beautiful a night to stay indoors, and as she looked up at the sky at the thousands and thousands of stars, she wished for...

It was so deep a wish she wasn't sure what it was. But she knew it had something to do with Dane. He'd worked at the clinic this morning, but he hadn't mentioned his plans for the rest of his day off. She told herself it didn't matter. But it did. She hadn't seen much of him since Sunday, and she wondered if her family had overwhelmed him.

Attuned to every sound in the silent night, she heard his terrace door open. The moon was almost full, and before she could call to him, he came striding over.

"What's this?" he asked, looking first at her and then at Allison and Jase's baby.

"I'm baby-sitting for a friend."

"Girl or boy?" He looked intrigued in spite of himself.

"This is Elizabeth. She's seven weeks old. And her mommy and daddy are enjoying a day to themselves for the first time since she was born. But I predict they'll be here shortly. Jase and Allison won't be able to stay away from her too long."

"I can understand that," Dane said, his voice husky as he continued to look at Elizabeth.

"Did you enjoy your afternoon off?" Maria asked, too curious not to ask.

"I went into Albuquerque and roamed the older section. I stopped in at the shop where your pots are displayed."

"How did you know which one it was?"

"Your mother mentioned it. I even bought one."

"Which one?"

"Come see," he said with a grin.

Standing, Maria shifted Elizabeth to the crook of her arm and followed him into his apartment. This particular pot was large, about two feet high, and sat on the floor next to his bookshelves. There were some dried flowers in it.

"It looks good there," Maria commented.

"The owner of the shop had it arranged like that and I wanted it as it was."

Maria knew this particular pot commanded a hefty sum, and she wondered why Dane had bought it. Did he just want a piece of her work? "I would have made you a pot, you know. You didn't have to buy one."

He shrugged. "I saw it, and I wanted it."

At the little-boy look on his face, she laughed. "Is that how you usually make your purchases?"

"Not only my purchases," he said, more seriously now. "I used to go after life that way, too."

"You will again," she said softly, knowing it was so. With everything that had happened to him, Dane might feel as if fate were controlling his destiny. But a man like him didn't let that happen for long. Choosing to move to Red Bluff proved it.

Just then Elizabeth began wiggling in Maria's arms and then let out a small cry. Not knowing how Dane would feel about being around a baby, Maria decided to make a suggestion anyway. "I have to get her a bottle. Would you like to come over for a little while? We can talk while she eats. I can't leave Sunny alone."

He seemed to debate with himself, but then agreed. "Sure. There's something else I got today that I want to show you. I'll bring it along."

As Elizabeth's cries grew stronger, Maria hurried over to her apartment and pulled the bassinet into her living room, laying the infant inside. While she went to fix the bottle, Elizabeth cried lustily. Maria smiled as she remembered how Sunny used to wail until she actually got that nipple between her lips.

Suddenly the crying ceased.

When Maria peeked into her living room, she saw Dane holding Elizabeth, quieting her, as he ran his finger along her small cheek.

"I couldn't stand to see her cry," he admitted.

It was obvious Dane cared deeply about children.

It was in his eyes and on his face every time he looked at one. But there was pain there, too, and Maria could hardly imagine losing a child.

She reached for the bottle that she'd just warmed and took it into the living room. "Would you like to feed her?" she asked.

But suddenly the pain in Dane's eyes became greater than his obvious caring. He shook his head and handed Elizabeth to her.

When Maria gazed up at him, she wanted him to know that she understood what he was going through. "I know seeing babies, even being around Sunny, is hard for you. On Sunday you must have felt as if there were kids everywhere." Her brothers and sisters had ten among them.

"There was so much happening on Sunday, the kids were just part of it. It wasn't so bad. But I did notice that your mom and dad don't seem to approve of our—" he searched for the word, then finished with, "—friendship."

"Is that what we have?" she asked casually.

"At least," he answered.

Their eyes locked, and Maria saw the desire he was keeping restrained and felt an answering lurch of it in herself. What would happen if his desire met hers? What would happen if they really let it explode?

The idea of the explosion made her so hot she could feel her cheeks flushing, and she said, "I'll take her now," to cover everything she was feeling.

After she sat on the sofa, Dane lowered himself beside her and picked up a book he'd laid on the end table.

As Elizabeth sucked on her bottle, Maria asked, "What's that?"

"Something I found at a little shop in Albuquerque—a used-book store." It was a leather-bound volume. There was no title on the cover. Dane opened it to the first page and held it so she could see.

"It's a journal!"

"Yes, it is. And look at the date."

"My goodness...1850. Have you read it?"

"I started to read it this afternoon. This Richard Chaplain crossed the United States in a wagon train with his wife and two daughters. They were on their way to California, but they came here instead."

"And you just found this in an old bookstore?"

"Yep. It was in a box that had come from an estate sale."

"It might be worth a lot, especially to a museum."

"It might be. When I'm finished reading it, I'll decide what to do with it. It's more fascinating than any novel I've read."

"Can I read it when you're finished?"

"Sure."

Again their gazes met and held.

Maria was so aware of the child in her arms, Dane at her elbow and the vibrations passing between them. But the vibrations were more than sensual electricity. A longing in this man seemed to reach out to a longing in her that she hadn't even known was there. It had to do with families and babies and a home.

Anticipation pulsed in the room along with a rippling excitement. Dane leaned toward her as if to kiss her, but then the sound of Elizabeth suckling on the bottle seemed to stop him. Something in his expression changed. His blue eyes suddenly weren't as warm, and she could see a screen of self-protection go up there.

Breaking eye contact, he stood, the old journal in his hand. "I'd better get going. I have some reading to do tonight."

"More of Richard Chaplain?" she managed to ask, although her heart was beating so fast it was hard to breathe.

"No. Medical journals." He crossed to her terrace door. "I'll see you at the clinic in the morning."

"Good night," she murmured softly as Dane let himself out.

She was left with the baby in her arms, but an emptiness in her heart. She needed Dane to fill it, but she wasn't sure if he was ready to.

Adding another chart to the stack on his desk Thursday afternoon, Dane was about to start writing patient notes when Joan rushed into the office. "I think we have an emergency out front. Frank Nightwalker cut himself badly on the blade of an ax."

"Bring him back to room two," Dane ordered, already lining up in his mind everything he'd need for the man.

Moments later Joan showed Frank Nightwalker to room two. He was a tall, husky man with long, gray hair held back with a leather thong. His features were strikingly Native American, and he was almost as pale as the white paper covering the examining table. He had his arm wrapped in a towel, but it was blood-soaked.

"Last tetanus shot?" Dane asked as he unwrapped the arm.

"Four years ago."

"How'd this happen?"

"I was felling trees, the ax slipped..."

Dane could see immediately that the gash needed to be sutured. But he also knew instantly that he couldn't do it. His fingers were too stiff for suturing, and he couldn't do that kind of procedure with his left hand.

Wrapping the arm again, he said to Joan, "Get Maria."

A half hour later Dane was sitting at his desk stewing about what had happened. He didn't even feel like a doctor when he had to call in someone else. He'd been naive to think that in general practice he wouldn't need full use of his right hand.

Staring at his hand and wrist, he remembered driving on the snow-covered road, the glow of headlights, the crash. Then as if it were yesterday, he also remembered waking up in the hospital, remembered not being able to use his hand for months. The frustration and the anger of it all built until the patient folders seemed to be a mockery of the practice he once had when he'd used the most technologically advanced medical equipment, dictation machines and had more staff than he knew what to do with. Sure he was helping patients here. But damn it! He didn't want to be limited. The limitations seemed to be bigger than life.

Furious with himself *and* fate, he pounded his damaged hand down on the desk in frustration.

In the ensuing silence, Maria's soft voice floated into the office. "Physical therapy would do a lot more good than damaging it further."

Her wise words, along with her beauty and his attraction to her, caused more frustration than all the rest of it, and he scowled at her. "I didn't ask for your opinion."

"No, but you obviously need it." She came into the office. "We could start tomorrow morning."

"But you have to take Sunny to your mother's."

"My mother won't mind my bringing her to the ranch a half hour early."

"Not even when she knows why?"

"Not even when she knows why. She wouldn't begrudge me helping you."

"I don't know, Maria...."

Coming closer to him, she was vehement. "Yes, you *do* know. I'll plan to meet you here tomorrow morning at seven-thirty unless you tell me differently." And then, she was gone, back to her patients.

Dane worked late, taking two walk-in patients so Maria could leave before him. And then, for the next two hours, he tediously wrote patient notes into the charts with his left hand.

When he left the clinic, he had supper at the Cantina, then drove back to his apartment. Restless, he settled down with Richard Chaplain's journal, becoming engrossed in hardships of another time, when life wasn't any kinder but seemed more simple. Before he turned off the light, he thought briefly about calling Maria, telling her to forget their morning appointment. But then he looked at his hand, thought about Frank Nightwalker and realized that if he didn't take the risk of hoping again, he might as well become a doctor without a practice.

On Friday morning he was at the clinic before Maria. He tried to distract himself by taking an inventory of the pharmacy, but he heard the door open and then he heard her footfalls in the hall. Leaving the clipboard in the supply closet, he went out to meet her.

She was wearing her usual jeans, but she'd paired

them with a cool-looking white eyelet blouse with a scooped neck and lace along its edge. Her necklace of coral and turquoise brought out the rich hue of her skin. Today she wore her hair in a high ponytail tied with a turquoise ribbon.

He'd rather kiss her than discuss therapy on his hand.

"What do we do first?" he asked, just wanting to get it over with.

"Let me get everything set up, then we'll get started."

He had no idea what she was going to set up, but he paced the office while he waited.

Finally Maria was ready. In the examination room she poked and prodded more thoroughly, asking him to move each finger, bend each joint, turn his wrist. Finally she pointed to a small vat sitting on the counter. It had a heating unit and was plugged into the receptacle.

She went over to it and checked the temperature gauge on the side. "This is melted paraffin. We're going to immerse your hand in it, and it will coat it like a glove. We'll give it about fifteen minutes. After that I'm going to work it a bit. Okay?"

"You seem to know what you're doing," he said gruffly.

While Maria caught up on odds and ends in the office, Dane sat in the examining room, his hand propped on a towel, waiting for the paraffin to work its magic while he tried to concentrate on a medical journal. Fifteen minutes later Maria was sitting in a chair before him, taking his hand gently into hers.

She carefully stripped off the paraffin and then had him bend his fingers again. He was surprised at how they seemed to be more flexible. As they sat in silence, Maria began working his fingers, the muscles in them, as well as those in the palm of his hand. It was almost like a massage, sensual and slow and sometimes deep. Her skin was so soft against his…so warm. She kept her gaze on his hand instead of looking at him, and he wondered if her touching him was as arousing for her as it was for him.

"I don't want to do too much or it'll get sore," she said finally, lifting her chin.

"I doubt that," he murmured. When his gaze caught hers, this time she didn't look away.

"After we're finished here, I'll give you some putty to work with to keep the muscles mobile. You might want to soak it at night and also work it like I am."

"I don't think I could do it like you are." His voice was raspy, and he couldn't keep his gaze from settling on her mouth.

Maria took a deep breath. "Dane…"

"Do you realize you have the most beautiful lips of any woman I've ever seen?" he asked, almost in bemusement.

Her eyes widened, her cheeks pinkened, and she shook her head gently, as if telling him they shouldn't be doing this.

But he was tired of standing still and feeling numb. He wanted to feel joy again and life and the spirit that Maria had inside of her. He only knew one way that he could truly feel that. Taking his hand from hers, he brought it to her face and gently traced the line of her brow with his thumb, feeling renewed circulation in his fingers, new hope in his hand. Touching her would get him through any treatment. Touching her could make life good again.

Maria strove to keep the yearning out of her eyes, off her face. But she didn't know if she was succeeding. She'd approached Dane this morning as a clinician would approach a patient. At least that's what she'd thought. But as she'd touched his hand, he wasn't just any patient. And as he touched her now, she certainly wasn't his doctor. There was too much of everything between them—desire, longing, differences, lifestyles, pasts.

But when Dane bent his head to her and nudged her forward, she couldn't back away. It was as if she was being drawn toward something so magical and special that to resist it was to turn away a gift. Dane's lips on hers were firm and possessive and questing. She leaned forward on her chair, and he took full advantage, drawing her up into his arms as he stood, pressing her close to him. When his tongue breached her lips, she touched it with hers, accepted his passion and gave back her own.

But when his hands went to the elastic band on her blouse and he pushed it up, she froze, put her hands on his and stopped him. She wasn't sure what Dane was looking for, but she knew it wasn't permanence. She knew it wasn't commitment. She guessed it wasn't anything other than pleasure that lasted for the moment.

That wasn't enough for her.

She finally realized she hadn't dated another man or started any kind of relationship with one because she was afraid he'd leave as Tony had. Tony's abandonment had made her feel worthless. His rejection of their child had thrown her into despair. When he'd chosen a career change instead of her, never even trying to reconcile, she'd felt as if their marriage had meant nothing. No, she hadn't reached out to him soon enough, but *he* was the one who'd left and easily replaced her with someone else.

What would keep another man from doing that?

Dane broke their kiss and stared down at her. "What's wrong?"

"The timing's wrong. *We* might be wrong. We hardly even know each other."

The nerve in his jaw worked. "I know enough."

"You don't even know if I've slept with a slew of men since my divorce," she returned, searching for anything to put a fence between them. But also knowing, after what she'd told him about herself, the quickly tossed boundary would mean nothing.

"You haven't slept with anyone since your divorce, have you?" he asked blatantly, as if he already knew the answer.

Her already warm cheeks seemed hotter. "No, I haven't."

The glaze of desire was still in his eyes as he smiled. "That settles that."

But she pulled out of his arms. "That settles nothing, Dane. I told you before—I'm not looking for an affair."

He stared at her long and hard. "And?" he asked prompting her.

"And I don't know if either of us is ready for more than that. But I do know I'm not going to let a physical therapy session turn into a make-out date." She was angry now at herself for letting this happen, at him for acting on what he was feeling.

His expression turned stony then, and she realized that as her anger ran hot, Dane's turned cold. "All right, I'll remember that."

Something in his voice alerted her to a change in him, in his attitude toward physical therapy. "Do you want to have another session?"

He moved his fingers, bending them a little farther than he had before. "Your treatment helped. I can tell. If we do five or six sessions, I'll be able to see whether it's a quick fix for the moment or more than that."

She met his gaze unwaveringly. "That's the point I was trying to make, Dane. I'm not a quick fix for the moment."

The silence stretched and pulsed between them. Finally he responded, "We're clear on that. But just remember something, Maria. It takes two to get those fires going, and you were every bit as involved as I was. Do you want me to come in early Monday morning, or would you rather have the session after work?"

Knowing she was as much to blame for everything that was happening between them as he was made her feel guilty that she'd reacted the way she had. "Morning is better. We never know how late we'll go in the evenings, and I like to get Sunny home." She paused for a moment, thinking about something else that could help Dane's hand. "I'll be out at the ranch Sunday afternoon if you want to try the potter's wheel. It would also be good therapy."

After a long silence he said, "Let me think about that. I'd better check my patient list. They'll be arriving shortly."

She nodded as if it didn't matter. She smiled as if she didn't care what Dane did.

After he left the exam room, Maria sank into the chair and took a huge breath. There was a reason she didn't pull away from Dane. There was a reason she was so drawn to him. She was falling in love with him.

What was she going to do about that?

It was almost six-thirty when Dane locked the clinic. Maria had left an hour ago.

Maria. Pretending there wasn't any electricity between them was as futile as him denying her manipulation of his hand didn't turn him on. All he had to do was get a whiff of her perfume. Was he hungering for her sexually simply because he couldn't have her? Or was the need becoming so great because satisfying it with her could fill his life in a way nothing else could?

As he opened the door to his SUV, someone called his name. He looked beyond the scraggly pines bordering the parking lot. Moments later Joe Youngbear emerged through them.

When Joe approached him, Dane said, "Maria left about an hour ago."

"I'm not looking for her. I wanted to talk to you."

That surprised Dane. "Do you want to come into the clinic? Are you having aftereffects from the knock on the head?"

Joe shook his head. "No problems from that. I wanted to ask you— You said something about knowing self-defense."

"Do you think you're going to need it?" Dane wondered what was brewing.

"I don't know. Trevor and his gang…they were snickering and saying some stuff when my friends and I passed them. I just want to be ready. You know what I mean?"

Dane nodded. "I know what you mean. But just remember fighting doesn't accomplish anything. Sometimes it makes matters worse." Dane felt he had to be clear on that with Joe.

"I know," the teenager said. "But I have to be able to hold my head up and get respect."

"I understand," Dane responded. And he did. It was why he'd suggested it. "Self-defense can enable you to do that. But you do have to practice."

"I will."

"It helps if you have a partner."

"Like you, you mean?"

"That's up to you. I can show you some moves, and then you can practice them with me or teach a friend. When did you have in mind?"

"How about now? I told my parents I was going out with some of my friends, and I am going to meet them later."

"Do you want to come back to my apartment?"

"I don't want to run into Maria. Can't we do it here?"

Dane thought about the reception area. "We can move the chairs around and make some space."

"I can pay you," Joe said.

Dane could see this might be a matter of pride. "Let's see how it goes, then you can tell me what you think it's worth to you. We can do it now if you'd like."

"You're sure?"

"Tamales can wait. A workout with you will be good for me."

Two hours later Dane sat in the Cantina and was having dinner, thinking about his self-defense class

with Joe. The boy learned quickly. He'd have no
problem defending himself. Dane had told Joe he
could meet him again at the clinic one night next
week, and they could practice again. In return for the
lessons, Joe was going to wash and wax his car tomorrow afternoon at the clinic when Maria wouldn't
be around.

On Friday night the Cantina was lively, and a
steady stream of customers came, ate and left. Dane
was finishing his tamales when he recognized Frank
Nightwalker passing by his table with a gray-haired
lady. Their gazes caught and met, and Frank stopped
after murmuring something to the woman.

"Are you acquiring a taste for tamales?" Frank
asked Dane with a smile.

"It looks like it." His gaze fell to Frank's arm. It
was sutured and looked as if it would heal nicely.
"I'm glad to see you're in better shape than the last
time I saw you."

"He scared the daylights out of me," the woman
said.

Frank took her hand and brought her up beside him.
"Dr. Cameron, this is Gloria Torres. Gloria, this is
Red Bluff's new doc, the one who works with Ma-
ria."

"It's good to meet you, Dr. Cameron," Gloria said.
"When Frank called me to tell me what he'd done, I
picked him up and drove him right to the clinic. You
and Dr. Youngbear took really good care of him."

"I think Dr. Youngbear deserves the credit for
that."

Frank said to Dane, "Gloria and I came out tonight
to celebrate."

Gloria held out her hand for Dane to see. There

was a diamond solitaire on her finger. "We're engaged," she said beaming from ear to ear.

"Congratulations," Dane said enthusiastically.

"We're throwing a party tomorrow night," Frank said. "If you're not doing anything, why don't you stop by? Lots of folks will be there you know already—Rod and Wyatt, Maria. My son's flying in tomorrow morning to help us celebrate. We'll have plenty to eat and drink. I'm on the west side of town, third ranch on the right."

Dane hadn't socialized much since coming to Red Bluff. Besides, if Maria was going... "It sounds like just what I need. What time?"

"Everybody's coming around eight. But whenever you get there is fine. We'll see you tomorrow night, then."

Music blared from a jukebox as Dane watched Frank and Gloria walk to their table. Frank put his arm around his fiancée, murmured something close to her ear and drew her into a tight hug. As they sat, they held hands.

The picture of Gloria and Frank stayed in Dane's mind as he paid his bill and drove back to his apartment. After he let himself inside, the silence seemed to pound around him. Going to his terrace, he stepped out and looked over to Maria's. She wasn't there, but he saw a light glowing in her bedroom.

Returning to his living room, he picked up the phone and dialed her number. She answered on the first ring.

"Maria, it's Dane."

"Hi. Is something wrong?"

"I hope I didn't wake you."

"No. I was watching an old movie."

"What old movie?"

She seemed to hesitate for a moment, but then she said, "*Roman Holiday*. I love Audrey Hepburn."

He was quiet for a few moments as he imagined her in bed, watching TV, her beautiful dark hair splayed across her pillow.

"I saw Frank Nightwalker at the Cantina tonight. He was with Gloria Torres and they told me they got engaged. They asked me to their party tomorrow night, and they mentioned you'd be there. I wondered if you'd like to go together."

After a pause she asked, "Like a date?"

"That's exactly what it would be." She was quiet for so long, he asked, "Maria?"

"I'm here."

"Are you worried about people talking?"

"No. I'm just wondering why you want to go on a date with me."

"Because I want to get to know you better outside of the clinic."

After another pause she said softly, "I'd like that, too."

"Good, then I'll stop by for you at a quarter of eight."

"A quarter of eight," she repeated.

"Good night, Maria."

"Good night."

When Dane put down the phone, he realized he was looking forward to tomorrow evening more than he'd looked forward to anything in a very long time.

Chapter Seven

As Dane stood with Maria on the porch at Frank Nightwalker's home, he felt young again and marveled at the feeling. Maria looked beautiful tonight in a teal and white gauzy sundress that fell gently over her breasts and gathered into a skirt that went almost to her ankles. The spaghetti straps of her dress were a tease, and ever since she'd opened her door to him, he'd imagined pushing them over her shoulders. Her hair fell down her back, swinging as she moved. The inclination to gather her into his arms was so strong.

But as Frank Nightwalker answered his door, Dane pushed the urge aside.

"Howdy, you two," the older man said. "It's good to see you. Come on in." As soon as they stepped into the great room, Frank swept them along toward a love seat where Gloria was talking to a couple.

"This is my son and daughter-in-law, Mac and Dina," Frank said with a smile.

The couple rose, and Dane saw that Frank's son

bore a striking resemblance to him, although Mac's hair was black. Dina hugged Maria and then so did Mac, and Dane realized that they already knew each other.

Frank explained to him, "Mac and Dina visit as often as they can. They live in Maryland."

"A long way from Red Bluff," Dane noted.

Maria was asking Dina, "Frank told me Kristen is running all of you ragged. Is she in bed?"

Dina explained to Dane, "Kristen's our daughter. She's sixteen months old now and doesn't know the meaning of stop or bedtime. Thank goodness traveling tuckers her out. She just went to sleep before the first guests arrived."

Just then a boy of around nine, who looked very much like Dina, came over to them. "Hey, Dad. Sheriff McGraw says I can see the jail tomorrow. Will you take me?"

Mac laughed and ruffled the boy's hair. "Sure, I will."

"And while you're there," Dina suggested, "Kristen and I can visit Allison and the new baby."

Shaking his head, Frank laughed. "I thought you came out here for a vacation."

After Mac surrounded Dina's waist with his arm, he drew her close to him. "This *is* a vacation. The fun part is visiting with all the friends we've made here as well as helping you and Gloria celebrate."

Dina addressed Maria again. "I want to show you the sketches I did in my last design class. One of them won an award."

Dane watched Maria's animated expression as she congratulated Dina and noticed the proud look on Mac's face.

Leaning close to Dane, Frank advised him, "Just jump right in. There's drinks in the kitchen and plenty of food in the dining room. In a little while we'll turn on some music out on the patio."

"You're a lucky man," Dane said sincerely, "to have so many people who want to celebrate with you."

"Don't I know it! It wasn't always this way, though. A few years ago I didn't even know my son. I'd left Mac and his sister and his mother when he was a kid. Then he met Dina and her son, and he started questioning why I'd left and whether he wanted to know me or not."

"Jeff's not Mac's son?"

"Oh, no. But you'd never know it, would you? Oh, I don't mean in physical looks. That's not what matters. There'll never be a rift between the two of them like there was between me and Mac." Glancing fondly at his son and daughter-in-law again, Frank added, "When Mac found Dina, his whole life changed. A good woman can do that."

Warming to the subject, Frank nodded to a tall man in jeans and a Western-cut shirt. "Take Jase McGraw over there." There was a pretty blonde beside the man in jeans, holding a baby. Dane realized it was the same child that Maria had baby-sat.

"Jase came here from Richmond," Frank went on, filling Dane in. "He and Allison had been friends for a long time. She came out for a visit, and look at them now—a family in the making."

Gloria came over to Frank and slipped her arm around his waist. "Why don't we turn on the music on the patio. I heard two more cars pull in. Pretty soon people will start spilling out there."

"Good idea." He and Gloria excused themselves.

A few minutes later Dane easily found himself falling into a conversation with Mac. After a short while Jase McGraw joined them. It was odd, but Dane felt comfortable with the two men as they talked about the area and the differences between living on the East Coast and living in the Southwest. But even while he was talking to them, he kept an eye on Maria as she mingled. She knew everyone, and he supposed that's what happened when doctors practiced in a community like this.

As the evening wore on, Dane realized this wasn't exactly what he'd expected from a "date". Though he enjoyed talking with everyone, he wanted to be with Maria. Searching her out, he asked if she was hungry. When she agreed that she was, they filled their plates at the buffet table and migrated out to the patio where they settled on a swing, their shoulders, hips and knees brushing.

"I can see why you didn't want to leave Red Bluff," Dane admitted.

"Exactly what do you see?" she asked in that get-to-the-bottom-of-it way of hers.

"You belong. I imagine it would be very hard to leave that. Not only do you have family, but you have a community of people who are like *more* family."

She nodded. "It's always been this way for me. Tony never really became a part of it, even though my family accepted him. It didn't seem to matter."

"Maybe it takes someone who doesn't have a large family to appreciate all of it."

When she looked up at him, her gaze was speculative.

Before she could analyze what he'd said, he took

her almost empty plate from her and set it down on the patio beside his. Then he stood and reached for her hand. "Let's dance."

The music was slow and sentimental, befitting an engagement party. Gloria and Frank were dancing, as were a few other couples. Dane took Maria into his arms naturally...wanting her there...as if she belonged there.

She gazed up at him with a mixture of surprise and amusement. "I guess this *is* a date."

When she smiled at him, he pulled her a little tighter. "That's what I said it was going to be."

With a soft sigh Maria settled against Dane, wishing she knew what he was thinking. He'd been looking at her differently tonight. She couldn't quite put her finger on how. It was as if something had changed in their relationship. He was more possessive, more claiming. As they danced, guests filled the patio, but Dane didn't break his hold.

Wyatt Baumgardner smiled and waved at them from the sidelines, but Dane murmured in Maria's ear, "Don't think you're going to be dancing with him tonight."

"That wouldn't be an order I'm hearing, would it?" she asked with amusement, remembering dancing with Wyatt at the chili cook-off, knowing that had been nothing like the thrilling feeling of dancing within Dane's embrace.

Dane's face was suddenly devoid of humor as he asked, "Would you rather be dancing with Wyatt or with me?"

If there was any time for honesty, it was now. "I'd rather be dancing with you."

The silver lights in Dane's blue eyes sparked her

own desire, and she knew if she wasn't careful they'd have a full-fledged fire to deal with.

Maria discovered that Dane was a superb dancer and though he didn't know the Texas two-step, he soon learned it. He looked younger tonight, more carefree than she'd ever seen him. As she felt the pressure of his fingers on her back, she wondered if the change in him was because of the physical therapy and getting increased use of his fingers and hand. It was as if he was hopeful again. But she knew with that hope came the probability that he wouldn't be staying. After all, a pediatric cardiologist of his caliber didn't bury himself in a small town in a general practice if he could help it. If Dane ever decided to embrace life again, he'd be gone. She held no illusions about that.

As the night wore on, she and Dane danced, sat on the swing sipping sodas, gazing at each other every now and then as they talked in low tones about whatever came into their heads. There was a level of comfort, excitement and attraction that she'd never felt with anyone before. He seemed so much like her, yet so different. It also seemed as if he was becoming a part of her. But she knew that might be only a dream in her own mind.

Some of the party-goers began leaving. Maria felt as if she were in another world as she and Dane danced to another slow ballad. As she laid her cheek against his chest, his strong arms locked around her waist, and she twined hers about his neck. When she looked up at him, there was no doubt that he was enjoying tonight as much as she was.

"Let's take a walk," he murmured in her ear, and

she nodded, also feeling a need to get away from the few remaining people.

The cooler air enveloped them as they strolled away from the lights and the people. Bluffs and cliffs loomed beyond the craggy earth, cactus and fence. Maria loved the rawness of the land here, the earth tones, turquoise sky and expansiveness. But as Dane slipped his arm around her shoulders, it was obvious he wasn't thinking of the landscape and neither was she. When they neared the fence line, they could hear the soft whinny of horses, but couldn't see them in the black night. Dane kept her standing by him, far out of the reach of the barn light.

"It's a nice party," Dane commented.

"Gloria and Frank are great people. They've both been lonely for a long time. I'm glad they found each other."

Dane was silent for a while, then took her elbow and turned her to face him. "When we were dancing, all I could think about was kissing you."

The huskiness in his voice, the intensity on his face, made her breathless. But she managed, "Why didn't you?"

"I was thinking about your reputation...and the gossips."

"My reputation and the gossips don't seem important right now," she murmured.

She'd been wanting to kiss him, too...to feel again the wonderful excitement of sharing more than words and a simple touch. His kisses could become addictive, something that were necessary for her to go on. The thought terrified her. Yet as he bent his head, the terror transformed into anticipation and longing and dreams that had long seemed out of her reach.

When Dane took her lips tonight, he wasn't the skilled doctor—he was a hungry man. She recognized the hunger because she was feeling it herself. Her arms slid under his and he brought her closer, kissing her ravenously, passing his hand over the bare skin of her shoulders. Then he was sliding the strap of her dress to the side, and the kisses became satin petals from her lips across her cheek down her neck.

Brushing her hair aside with his jaw, he said in a rasping voice, "You smell so good and you taste so good."

She stroked the muscles in his back. "You do, too," she murmured, lost in him, lost in the sensuality of whatever was happening between them.

But when his lips nipped her shoulder and when his hand came to rest on her breast, palming it, giving her pleasure as she'd never known before, she knew she had to stop this. Unless Dane had changed his mind. Unless Dane...

She backed out of his caress and fortified herself with a deep breath, trying to clear her head and her heart. "What's tonight all about, Dane?"

He looked angry for a moment. "It's about being together and enjoying it."

"But we've gone beyond conversation and dancing."

"Isn't that what's supposed to happen on a date?" he asked politely. The anger seemed to be gone now, or else it was just simmering below the surface.

"We covered this subject before," she said. "I guess it depends on the woman you're dating. I told you I don't believe in going to bed with a man at night and leaving him in the morning. I'm just not like that."

"And what about *not* leaving him in the morning?" Dane demanded. "What about simply enjoying each night for what it is, taking life day by day, not looking for more than what you've got right now?"

Maria shook her head. "I wasn't raised that way."

That simmering anger came to the surface again. "That's a cop-out, Maria. Maybe you're just afraid to take a little adult pleasure, to forget you're a mother and a daughter and to remember you're a woman."

The words were harsh, and Maria felt the acute sting. She didn't cry often, but she felt like crying now...for all the things she wanted and couldn't have, for Dane's idea of what they had together. Although she was never usually at a loss for words, in the starlit night, with the moon golden, tears were too close to the surface for her to speak. She didn't want them to fall, and if they did, she certainly didn't want Dane to see them.

Spinning on her heel, she turned away from him and tried to keep her walk from becoming a run.

"Maria," he called impatiently.

But she wasn't stopping. He could think what he wanted about her. But she knew her heart. It wouldn't survive a one-night stand with Dane, or a three-night stand. She wanted so much more than that.

Dane walked down the path to Maria's workshop on her parents' ranch late Sunday afternoon, unsure what he was doing here.

Last night, when Maria had run from him, he'd been angry and confused. Angry, he supposed, because he was sexually frustrated. Confused because Maria wasn't the type of woman to run. She usually

stood her ground and made her point. But maybe she
had made her point and that's why she'd gone. Or
maybe what he'd said had hurt her.

They hadn't talked on the ride home, and they'd
gone to their separate apartments more like strangers
than two people who'd been in each other's arms a
half hour before. He supposed he'd come this afternoon because he didn't want to work in the clinic
tomorrow with all that tension between them.

But as soon as he stood in the doorway of Maria's
workshop and saw her at her workbench, he knew
exactly what he'd come for—to deliver an apology.

When she looked up, she was smiling, obviously
intending to see one of her family. Her smile vanished
when she saw him, and she went back to her painting.
She was stroking a desert scene onto a high-necked
pot, and obviously thought more of that pot at this
moment than she did of him.

"Do you mind if I come in?" he asked.

When she glanced up at him this time, he could
read no expression on her face. That was unusual.

"I'm working," she said matter-of-factly.

"Your mother told me that. But you'd invited me
here today—"

"You came to use the potter's wheel?" There was
a light of interest in her eyes now.

"I don't know about that."

She picked up her brush again. "If you came to
use the wheel, I'll show you. If you didn't, I don't
have time for...anything else."

So much for her letting him back into this grace-
fully. "Maria."

She didn't look at him.

"I'm sorry about last night."

Still she didn't look up. "Sorry about what, Dane? Not convincing me to go further? Sorry you couldn't convince me that I should want to jump into bed with you and forget my values? Forget the code I've lived by?"

This was the Maria he knew, and although he didn't always like her bald-faced honesty, he preferred it to her silence. "I'm sorry if I upset you or hurt you. I *do* respect how you live your life." And then he was honest, too. "I wanted you badly, and I couldn't see beyond that."

"And now?" she asked softly, finally gazing up at him without the guardedness.

"And now...although I still want to take you to bed, I'd rather just enjoy your company."

After her eyes passed over every detail of his face, after he felt as if she were looking inside his soul, she asked, "And you want to use the potter's wheel?"

"Is that the only way I can stay?" he asked with wry amusement.

A smile finally twitched up the corners of her mouth. "Yes."

He shrugged. "Whatever it takes."

A short time later, Maria had shown Dane how to position himself behind the potter's wheel. She picked up a hunk of clay and handed it to him. "If your clay isn't centered, when you begin to pull up the piece, it will be off balance. You'll be fighting it. As you're holding it, it's important to use your whole body. This is great for keeping the neck and shoulders in shape."

Then she turned on the wheel and said, "Okay, let's give it a try. Throw the clay down close to the center of the wheel. You want it to really stick."

Dane thought this was a little like making mud pies and smiled at the comparison.

"Keep your hands on the clay, and as the wheel spins, pat it into a cone, forcing it into the center of the wheel."

When he did as Maria directed, he realized it took his whole body to do it. This was a lot more physical than he'd imagined.

"Now set your hands on the clay," she said, "and force it into the center."

Instinctively he used his left hand as a guide and pressed down with his right, forcing the clay into a cone.

"You're doing great."

He could easily see how this was going to work the muscles in his hand and his wrist, strengthening them.

Using the force of his body to keep his arms from moving with the clay, he worked a while longer. "I'll bet you're stronger than you look, if you do this often," he teased.

"You wouldn't want to meet me in a dark alley," she agreed with a smile.

After his beginning success, Dane had several mishaps when the clay went off center or he pressed incorrectly. But as he worked the clay for a while, he learned how to pull up the walls of the pot. The faster the wheel spun, the faster he could pull up. But when he moved too fast, the pot fell apart, off center, and he had to start over again.

Maria directed him what to do, and when he caught on, she sat at her workbench, continuing what she'd started.

About an hour later Dane had fashioned a piece

that almost resembled a vase. The muscles of his hand truly felt worked and were tired, but there was a satisfaction in that.

Maria used a wire to cut the bottom of the pot from the wheel and set it on one of the tables. "It needs to sit until it's leather hard," she told him. "Then you can trim it and make some adjustments."

"You mean it's not done?"

She laughed. "That depends on—"

Just then Sunny came running into the workshop. When she saw Dane, she made a beeline toward him and stood between his knees looking up at him.

He had clay on his hands and he said, "Whoa there. I'm going to get you all messed up."

But she looked up at him with her beautiful brown eyes and asked, "Ice cweam?"

Before today looking at Sunny had caused him pain and reminded him of Keith. But now he just saw the bright little girl she was. Wrapping his arm around her, he drew her up onto his lap. "Ice cream, huh? If that's an invitation, it sounds pretty good to me."

An hour later Maria collected the ice cream dishes and took them into the kitchen. Dane had easily spoken to her parents and family while they'd enjoyed the ice cream. He'd listened intently as her father had told him about breeding Appaloosas, and he'd seemed interested as her mother had gone on about each of their children, their schooling and accomplishments.

The whole time, Maria had been a bit mystified.

She'd never expected to see Dane here today, never expected him to apologize. Last night his need had been clear, and her expectations had been too high. She'd thought that had been the end of it.

Did Dane simply want her friendship while he was in Red Bluff? Could they just be friends?

She understood his life was changing. When Sunny had come running to him, Maria thought he might ward her off or push her away. But he hadn't. He'd almost embraced her presence, and that was a big step for him.

Could he take an even bigger step? Could he open his heart to love again?

Maria had loaded the last dish in the dishwasher when her father came into the kitchen, leaned against the counter and crossed his arms over his chest.

She knew that stance. She'd seen it before. "What is it, Dad?"

"It's Dane Cameron," he said in a low voice so no one on the patio would hear.

"What about him?" she asked bluntly.

"Are you sure you want to get involved?"

"What makes you think I'm involved?"

Her father snorted. "Daughter, I know you. I see how he is with you, how he looks at you, and how you look at him."

Maria shook her head. "He won't be staying in Red Bluff."

"You know that for sure?"

"I know that once he's over his grief, once he gets back the use of his hand, he might leave even faster than he came."

"But you don't want him to leave." Her father's gaze was as penetrating as his stance was attentive.

"No," she responded, telling him the truth as she always had.

"He's not like us, Maria."

As much as she appreciated her mother and father's

old ways, she also became frustrated by them sometimes. "Tony was like us, Dad, and he left me, with
hardly a second thought. So don't tell me about Dane
not being like us and try to convince me that matters."

"Are you sure you're not just rebelling?" Tom Eagle almost scolded.

"Rebelling against what you and Mom have taught
me? Rebelling against everything I hold dear and
love? No, I'm not rebelling. Dane has nothing to do
with rebellion. There's this connection between us
I've never felt with anyone before."

Her father's eyes were troubled. "I don't want you
to get hurt again."

She took a deep breath, thought about it, then answered, "I don't *want* to get hurt again. But I can't
just shut off what I'm feeling for Dane."

"Even if he can shut off what he feels for you?"

Suddenly she realized she wanted to explore whatever she *might* be able to have with Dane. "Yes. I
don't know what's going to happen, Dad."

"I never could get you to listen to common sense,"
he grumbled.

She crossed over to him and gave him a hug. "No,
you never could. But you're always here when I
don't. Thanks for that."

Her father patted her on the back as he had when
she was a child, and she almost felt like crying again.
Dane had stirred up too many emotions, some she
hadn't felt in years, and she didn't know if she'd ever
get the lid back on all of them again.

On Monday morning, after Dane's physical therapy
session, Maria drove to the Albuquerque General

Hospital. She had several patients from Red Bluff who were there, and she would make rounds before starting her afternoon hours at the clinic. She thought about yesterday at the ranch with Dane, and her conversation with her father. She was getting in deeper and deeper and she knew that. But she'd always followed her heart and she couldn't change the way she met life now. She was more than a little in love with Dane, and she didn't know how she was going to handle it.

After examining her patients' charts, she visited Mrs. Gundale, who'd broken her hip on Saturday and had been rushed to Albuquerque. She was stable, disgruntled at what had happened to her and worried about going home. Then there was Al Ramirez, who'd fallen off a ladder and ended up with a broken leg and a concussion. He'd be discharged tomorrow. Bea Davis was another matter. She was having surgery for breast cancer today, and Maria spent the most time with her.

It was almost eleven when Maria returned her patients' charts to the nurses' desk. As she was dropping them into their cart, she glimpsed Dr. Grayson, a cardiologist who'd helped her with many of her patients. On impulse she hurried and caught up to him.

"Hello, there," he said when he saw her. "I haven't bumped into you for a while. How's everything going at the clinic?"

Dr. Grayson was in his sixties with salt-and-pepper hair, a round, cherubic face and gray eyes that could see much more than symptoms. He'd respected her from the start of her work at the clinic so she felt a fondness for him as well as respect.

"It's good. Dr. Grover officially retired and we found a replacement."

He looked pensive for a minute, then snapped his fingers. "That's right. Somehow you snared that ace cardiologist from New York. What's his name? Dane Cameron?"

"Yes, that's it."

"How's he working out? Sometimes specialists going into general practice have a problem."

"He's working out just fine."

"And why did he come to Red Bluff? It seemed a little suspicious to me that a surgeon of that caliber would want to practice in a small town—unless he was hiding from something."

"Grieving, not hiding. He lost his wife and son and was injured in the accident. His hand. That's why he's trying general practice."

Dr. Grayson's face took on a sympathetic expression. "That's rough. But you said he's working out all right?"

"Just fine. But sometimes I think he misses his specialty. So I was wondering if you ever need a consult with your pediatric patients?"

Dr. Grayson grinned. "Maria, you know I can always use a good consult. In fact, I have a premature baby right now who has me worried. It was serendipitous that we should talk today. Do you think Dr. Cameron would mind if I give him a call?"

"The truth is, I don't know if he'll mind. He doesn't know I'm talking to you."

"Then why *are* you talking to me?"

"Because I want to see Dane happy."

"Hmm. You're more than colleagues?"

She felt her cheeks redden. "I'm not sure. But I know I don't want to see his talent wasted."

"All right, then. I'll give him a call. But he'll wonder where I heard about him."

"You can tell him we ran into each other. I'm not hiding anything from Dane."

Except the fact that she was in love with him.

Chapter Eight

When Dane received the message from Betsy to call Dr. Grayson at Albuquerque General, he wondered what it was about. Between patients he dialed the number, and the doctor himself answered.

"Hello, Dr. Cameron," Dr. Grayson said in a booming voice. "I don't know if you know who I am, but I'm a cardiologist at Albuquerque General. I know your specialty was pediatric cardiology and I have a preemie I need a consult on. Do you think you could come up and take a look at her?"

Dane had seen Dr. Grayson's name mentioned in his patients' charts but he wondered how the doctor knew about him. "You know my credentials?"

"Well, yes. Through the articles you've published."

"But how did you know I was here in Red Bluff?"

"I spoke with Maria Youngbear this morning, and she told me."

"Do you mind telling me how my name came

up?'' He knew he was putting the doctor on the spot, but he didn't care.

''She mentioned you might be interested in consulting.''

''I see.''

''If you're not, I'll have to look farther afield.''

If he could help this preemie, he would. And Maria knew that. ''No, don't do that. I'll be glad to come in and consult with you. How about tomorrow morning?''

''That would be fine. Around eight o'clock?''

''See you then.''

Dane's temper was hot and getting hotter as he put down the receiver. When he saw Maria pass by the office door on her way to an examining room, he snagged her arm. ''I need to talk to you.''

She followed him into the office. ''What's wrong?''

''I just got a phone call from Dr. Grayson. Seems to me I was the topic of your discussion this morning.''

She looked chagrined for a moment. ''When I saw him today…I just thought you might want to stay involved with your specialty.''

''Seems to me that's *my* decision to make, not yours. If I wanted to put out the word I was consulting again, I'd do it.''

Part of his frustration with her came from spending time with her yesterday as well as in their PT session this morning, and yet not kissing her or touching her, not being really close. They'd acted like friends because that had seemed to be the best, but there was a lot lacking in that. Now when he looked at her, he became aroused again, and the urge to kiss her and touch her was so strong he almost forgot why he'd called her into the office.

When he moved a few steps closer to her, she didn't back up but stood her ground. "With the use of your fingers returning, I thought you'd want to stay active in your field. You seem to be better with Sunny now..."

"Maria." Her name was a puff of exasperation. "Sometimes you go too far, and sometimes you don't go far enough." Then he took her face between his hands, claimed her lips with his and kissed her with pent-up frustration and overwhelming desire.

He felt her breath of surprise. But then she was responding to him, lacing hands in his hair, kissing him back as desperately as he was kissing her. He caressed the lines of her face, delved his fingers into her beautiful long hair and passed his hands down her body. It was such a beautiful curving body, and the idea of her breasts under his lips set him on fire. They could have been on top of a mountain. They could have been in the middle of Times Square. It wouldn't have mattered, because their passion couldn't be denied now, not by either of them. He felt that in her, and he knew it in himself, too. They'd been heading for this from the day they'd met.

When he pushed her lab coat from her shoulders, she shrugged out of it and then she helped him with his. There was a wild, frenzied need about everything they did as their fingers tangled, their lips melded, and he reached behind him to lock the door, then walked her backward to the sofa. He took her down there, unbuttoning her blouse at the same time, murmuring her name, letting the out-of-control, restless feelings take over. He'd controlled all of it for much too long.

Maria's sighs and soft moans drove him on. He finished with her blouse, unhooked her bra and bent his head to her breasts. Taking the tip into his mouth, he tongued it, caressing her midriff, stealing her sighs with his kiss. His name was a broken moan on her lips, and he knew he was pleasing her as well as himself.

Maria had never felt this fiercely wanton before. There was a mindless quality to it. Dane burned away her inhibitions, burned away traditions, burned away morals she'd lived with for a lifetime. He hadn't given her time to think, and that had been her undoing. The onslaught of the sensual electricity between them had been more than she could overcome with good sense and logical thought. The feel of his lips on hers, the hot wet texture of his tongue, his hands so large and powerful on her skin, sent her to a place where only feeling and pleasure mattered.

When she felt him fumble with the snap of her jeans and the zipper, she fleetingly wondered if she could please him…if she was enough. But the thought fled in helping him rid her of her jeans. She was practically naked on the sofa, and he was on top of her and there was nothing in the world she wanted more. She reached for the zipper on his fly, and when her hand caressed him, he groaned deep and guttural, and she found pleasing him was the most satisfying thing she'd ever done. He was so much stronger than she was, so much more powerful and so very hungry. But his power became hers, and she became as hungry as he was. A trembling began inside of her that could only be satisfied in one way—by a union with Dane.

She wasn't sure which of them heard the buzzing first. It seemed to come from somewhere far away. But it was insistent and didn't stop. She took a breath, opened her eyes and realized it was coming from the intercom on her desk.

Dane must have realized the same thing because he suddenly froze, then swore.

"We have to get it," she murmured.

"Don't I know it." His voice was deep and husky and every bit impatient. He pulled himself together first, got to his feet, and with the flaps of his shirt flying unbuttoned, he pressed the button on the intercom. "Yes, Betsy."

Maria could hear Betsy's voice. "Virgil Harrihan's wife brought him in. He's having chest pains radiating up to his jaw and down his arm."

"Don't try to bring him back here. I'll come out to the waiting room." Dane had already buttoned his shirt and tucked it into his jeans. "Don't move him," he added.

Maria had sat up while he was speaking to Betsy, pulled on her jeans, refastened her bra and buttoned her blouse with trembling fingers. She wondered how long it would be until her body stopped shaking, wondered how long it would be until she realized how foolish she'd almost been.

Dane was already out the door as she slipped into her sandals and scrambled to her feet, hurriedly following him.

Their gazes didn't meet as Dane grabbed aspirin from the supply room and pushed an examining table that served as a gurney to the waiting room. After one look at Virgil, his sweating and pale face, Dane ordered Betsy to call an ambulance. All of the other patients in the reception area seemed frozen as they watched and listened.

Quickly helping Virgil onto the gurney, Dane gave him the aspirin and then pushed him to an exam room where a portable heart monitor was located. Once there, Maria administered nitroglycerine under his tongue.

Less than fifteen minutes later, Dane had hopped into the ambulance with Virgil, and right behind them Betsy was driving Clara to the hospital.

Taking a few deep breaths, Maria returned inside, worried about Virgil, knowing she now had a waiting room full of patients to see. She reminded herself Virgil was in good hands.

Thinking about Virgil and the waiting patients helped her keep her mind off the interlude in her office when she'd been mindless with desire in Dane's arms. They hadn't really looked at each other since the intercom had buzzed. Maria didn't know if she felt embarrassed, awkward or simply foolish. And she had *no* idea what Dane was thinking and feeling.

It was almost four when Dane called from the hospital in Albuquerque. His voice was curt. "Virgil's EKG changes are marginal, and his condition improved with the nitro. So Dr. Grayson ordered serial enzymes."

That meant Dr. Grayson would check Virgil's cardiac enzymes every eight hours for twenty-four hours. The enzyme readings would dictate the next step— anything from a stress test to surgery.

Before she had a chance to comment, Dane continued, "I'm going to consult with Dr. Grayson about his preemie, then I'll be back."

The clinic's waiting room was still full. "I'll be

here,'' she said, knowing her mother wouldn't mind if she was late picking up Sunny, knowing she had to talk to Dane about what had happened earlier.

Maria had seen the last of the patients and was working in the office when Dane returned. When he came in, she put down her pen and stood.

"How did it go?" she asked him, finally meeting his eyes, finally seeing there the remembrance of what had happened on the sofa in their office.

"Virgil's stable and Clara's holding his hand. At the same time, she's scolding him for not taking care of himself."

Normally this would have made Maria smile. But not now. "And with Dr. Grayson?" she pressed.

"I gave him my opinion, but if you expect anything more to come of it, don't." Dane turned away from her and went to his desk.

But she wouldn't let it go. "How did it feel? Being back in your specialty, I mean?"

With an exasperated sigh, he looked at her again. "Even if I regain the use of my hand and fingers, I don't know if I want to go back to pediatric cardiac surgery. So stop pushing, Maria. Do you want me to leave Red Bluff? Is that why you're doing this?"

"No!"

His gaze was so piercing she wasn't sure what to say, but finally admitted, "You're great in the clinic with the patients, but you're capable of so much more. I think if you get back the use of your hand, the fire for what you used to do will come back."

"So you're trying to push me out before we get too...attached?"

Like watching a movie reel, she could see him above her on the sofa, feel his body weight on hers, remember the taste and fervor of each of his kisses. She'd fallen in love with him, yet she knew he'd be leaving. He was too good *not* to leave.

Thank God for that buzzer. If she'd made love with Dane, she didn't know if she could ever recover from his leaving.

"What happened in the office..." she began.

"Should have happened in my bedroom," he finished for her.

"It shouldn't have happened at all."

He shook his head. "That's some state of denial you're in. We want each other, Maria. It's not going to go away just because you think it should."

"I might want you," she confessed in a low voice. "But I'm going to do what's good for myself and for Sunny. And you're going to have decide if you want a real life or a temporary one."

His brows drew together, and anger lined his face. "What's *that* supposed to mean?"

"It means you can't hide out in Red Bluff forever. It means you're going to have to face whatever life you want for your future."

His voice went low and deep. "And what kind of life have you faced for your future? One without men? One without kissing and touching? One without sexual pleasure?"

"When Sunny's older—"

"When Sunny's older," he cut in, "you're going to have missed so much you won't know how to begin again."

Just standing here, six inches away from him, made her feel hot and bothered and excited like a teenager. Like a woman. But she had to do what was right for her, even if that hurt, even if she wanted something else.

What Dane needed was a good dose of hope to help him heal, to help him move forward. And she thought of a way she might be able to help put his life in perspective.

"What are you doing on Wednesday?" she asked.

"Why?" he returned warily.

"Will you spend the afternoon with me? There's someplace I'd like you to see."

"You want me to be a tourist?" he asked wryly.

"Not exactly. You'll understand when we get there."

"I don't like mysteries, Maria," he told her with narrowed eyes.

"It's not a mystery. It's a surprise. If Allison can find a baby-sitter, maybe she'll come into the clinic, field calls for us and only page us if it's absolutely necessary. What do you think?"

"I don't suppose you're taking me to see a motel somewhere."

The anger was gone now, and a hint of amusement in his voice told her that they weren't enemies, that they were more than friends. "The opposite from a motel, actually."

He gave her a puzzled look, then shook his head. "I'm not even going to try to imagine what. All right. I'll go with you to this mysterious place for one reason—I like spending time with you."

And she liked spending time with him. But she wasn't sure they had much time left before their lives took different roads.

"Is it much farther?" Dane asked on Wednesday afternoon, with a sideways glance at Maria. Last eve-

ning he'd given Joe a second self-defense class and
had considered quizzing the teenager about where his
sister might be taking him. But then he'd decided
against it. She had her reasons for keeping the desti-
nation to herself.

He and Maria had made rounds in Albuquerque
before starting out. Virgil had had a stress test, a heart
catheterization and angioplasty. He was being released tomorrow. Clara had hugged them both, re-
lieved, hopeful she and Virgil would have many more
years together.

Dane had insisted on driving today, even though
he didn't know where Maria was taking him. She'd
given him directions to Chimayo, about forty miles
northwest of Santa Fe in the Sangre de Cristo Moun-
tains.

Now, as they finally drove through the town, Dane
just arched his brows. There wasn't much of it.

Maria guided Dane until they ended up at El Santuario de Chimayo.

"You brought me to a church?" he asked with
some small astonishment.

"It's not just *any* church," she scolded. "This is
called the Lourdes of America."

Dane sent her an odd look. "As in miracles?"

She nodded.

He gave a desultory glance around at the site where
there was a restaurant, a gift shop and a food stand.

"Try to look beyond all that," she advised him,
and opened her door.

As they walked toward the adobe mission, she gave
him its background. "In 1810 a friar saw a light on
a hillside. Going to that spot, he found a crucifix. A

local priest took the crucifix to Santa Cruz, but it kept disappearing and was found back in its place on the hillside. So a small chapel was built there. People started coming to see the crucifix, then the miracles began. There were so many that this mission took its place.''

"And why did you bring me here?" he asked.

"By the time we're finished, I think you'll understand."

Dane didn't like mysteries or anything he couldn't see, touch and feel. The crucifix on the chapel altar didn't look all that mysterious. The dirt pit where it had been supposedly found was an open hole behind the main altar.

It was the prayer room near the pit that captured all of Dane's attention. He'd seen pictures of shrines where crutches and braces and canes hung on the walls in testament to the miracles that had occurred. But being here like this, seeing them actually before him, gripped him in a way he didn't understand.

He glanced to his side at Maria who was standing with her eyes closed and her head bowed before the wall of crutches. She was wearing a white dress today. It was cotton, fitted at the waist, flaring to her ankles. She looked like an angel. And maybe she was.

She'd brought him here for a reason, and he could see it now. He took another long look at the crutches, the braces, the handmade shrines. Then he examined his hand and his fingers, and he moved them, not perfectly, but much better than he had a few weeks ago. He didn't need a miracle...at least not the way these other folks had. If he wanted the use of his hand back, he'd have to work at it, he'd have to want it, he'd have to realize nothing could bring back his family.

It had been years since he'd said a prayer, even longer still since he'd really believed. But standing here beside Maria today, he prayed with a faith that was tentative, but there nonetheless. More than having his hand be whole again, he needed his heart to be whole. He wasn't sure how even a higher power could make that possible, but he vowed to be open to *letting* it happen.

The drive home to Red Bluff was silent, and Maria wondered if Dane was thinking about everything he'd seen, or if he just wanted to get back to his life as he knew it.

On the outskirts of the town Dane asked her, "Do you want to stop for supper at the Cantina before we pick up Sunny?"

"Sure," Maria responded, glad he was finally talking to her. She had no idea what was going on in his head, and maybe over dinner he would tell her.

Midweek the Cantina wasn't quite as busy as on weekends. The hostess showed them to a table.

Dane took the menus from behind the salt and pepper shakers and handed one to Maria.

But she didn't open it. Instead she asked him, "Are you angry with me for taking you to El Santuario?"

"Why do you think I'd be angry?"

She shrugged. "Churches aren't everyone's cup of tea. You might be thinking it was presumptuous of me to think a church could make any kind of difference to you."

He rested his elbows on the table and studied her for a moment. Then he said, "I did think that when we first got there."

"And then?"

"And then I realized exactly why you'd taken me there. You thought I needed a dose of hope, a reality check, to convince me my circumstances are darn good compared to others. I'm physically healthy, I have a career, I have a life if I want it. Maybe I needed to see all that. But if you expected a miracle, that I'd suddenly know exactly where I'm supposed to go or what I am supposed to do or be...that didn't happen."

She shook her head. "I didn't expect a miracle. I did want you to see that you have a lot to be grateful for. I know you've lost a lot, Dane. I'm not denying that. But you won't get any of it back by not moving forward."

After a brief silence he nodded. "If nothing else, I know I need to take the physical therapy seriously. It was self-pity that kept me from doing it before."

"Don't be so hard on yourself. Healing *does* take time...even for a doctor."

Gazing into her eyes, he asked, "Are you trying to get me to move forward so you can push me out of your life?"

"Dane..."

"I think it's time you look at the truth, too, Maria. Sure it would be messy if we have an affair and then I leave. But wouldn't it be worth knowing each other like that?"

Everything inside her told her that any time with Dane would be worth the heartache. But something else deeper urged her to say, "We're very different, Dane. What you just said proves it. I can't imagine an affair. I believe in commitment and walking a road with one person."

He didn't look angry, but he did look frustrated. "You didn't have any affairs before you met your husband?"

Her cheeks heated, but she shook her head and told Dane the truth. "I was a virgin when I married Tony. He was patient with me, and we waited until our wedding night to consummate our relationship. I was raised that way, Dane. What almost happened in our office the other day terrified me. How could I let passion override everything I believe?"

Now he leaned back, putting distance between them. "Are you telling me you want me to stay away from you?"

Distance was the last thing she wanted. But leading him on wasn't fair, either. "I don't know. I guess to you I seem very naive."

"I'm not sure what you seem to me."

His voice was deep and husky, and she felt like crying.

The waitress came to the table then, and they quickly looked over the menu and ordered. Composing herself, Maria tried to get above her deep feelings for Dane as they talked of other things. But as they ate, there was tension between them again because she wanted nothing more than to lie in Dane's arms. Yet she knew she couldn't do that unless he loved her...unless he wanted to spend his life with her.

They skipped coffee and dessert. Neither seemed to have the desire to linger. After Dane drove to her parents' ranch, Carmella opened the door to them, smiling, asking how their day had been.

Maria's father was watching TV and he switched it off. Sunny was curled on the sofa beside him, sleeping. He brushed his granddaughter's hair back from her forehead. "She managed to stay awake till about ten minutes ago." His smile disappeared when his gaze rested on Dane. "You had a good trip to Chimayo?"

"I'd never seen anything like it before," Dane responded with a respect in his voice that told the Eagles he appreciated the history of the shrine.

Carmella asked, "Can I get you something to eat or drink?"

"We stopped at the Cantina, Mom," Maria told her. "I think we'd better get Sunny home."

"Before you go, I have something I want to ask you." Maria's mother addressed Dane. "Tom and I are celebrating our thirty-fifth wedding anniversary on Sunday. We're having a party and we'd like you to come."

"Congratulations," Dane said. "And thank you for inviting me. I'd be honored to celebrate thirty-five years of marriage with you. That's some feat."

"After we married, we grew up together," Tom explained. "I think it's much easier that way than waiting until you're older to marry and being set in your ways. That's probably why younger folks these days have so much trouble. Too much selfishness. Not enough compromise."

Although Maria knew her father hadn't meant it that way, he'd described her marriage to Tony. Both of them had been selfish in their way, and she'd been unwilling to compromise until it was too late.

Dane must have sensed what she was thinking and stepped into the awkwardness. Crossing to the sofa, he offered, "I'll carry Sunny out to the car."

Then he scooped the toddler up into his arms as if it were the most natural thing in the world. The sight of him holding her daughter hurt Maria now because she could see so clearly a vision of the family they could be.

At the parking lot to their apartment building, Dane took Sunny from the car and carried her to Maria's door. Maria unlocked it, and they went inside. Taking Sunny to her bedroom, he laid her in her crib.

She mumbled, "Nighty-night," and he smiled, brushing his hand over her cheek.

No matter what Dane had said about not being around enough for his son, Maria knew he would be a wonderful father.

Her mom had dressed Sunny in her pajamas before she'd fallen asleep on the couch. So Maria now kissed her daughter good-night and closed the door partway.

Following Dane into the living room, she asked, "Would you like a cup of coffee?"

But he shook his head. "It's probably better if I don't stay."

She knew he was right. But she wanted him to stay so much more than she wanted him to go...so much more than she wanted to do the right thing. She followed him to the door.

"What can I get your parents for their anniversary?" he asked.

"They won't expect a gift."

"Thirty-five years of marriage deserves a lot more than a gift. Is there anything they particularly like?"

She thought about it for a moment. "They like big band music. Maybe a CD?"

"That's easy enough."

They stood gazing at each other then. Maria wanted to say so many things, yet she couldn't hold Dane where he didn't want to be. She couldn't convince him he was ready for a new life if he wasn't.

The silence became loud in the dimly lit living room, and Dane broke eye contact. "I'll see you in the morning."

When he opened the door to leave, she touched his arm. "Dane..." Tears burned in her eyes and she felt foolish.

He touched her then. He brushed the back of his knuckles along her cheekbone, then let his hand drop to his side. "I want to kiss you, Maria. But we both know I want more than a kiss, and I think my self-control has about run out where you're concerned. Thank you for today. It's something I'll always remember." Then he stepped out into the hall and closed her door.

Maria leaned against it and let the tears come. She loved Dane Cameron with all her heart. But she wanted *his* heart in return. She couldn't accept his desire in place of his love, not and be true to who she was.

She felt more alone at this moment than she'd ever felt in her life.

Chapter Nine

Dane stood at his terrace door looking out over the landscape, sipping a cup of instant coffee. He had a few extra minutes this morning, since he was going directly to Red Bluff High School to do sports physicals. Last night had been filled with dreams of what had been...and what could be. It had been hard as hell to leave Maria in her apartment alone—to come back to his apartment alone.

The phone rang, startling him. Not that many people had his number.

When he picked up the receiver and said hello, a brusk voice asked, "Dr. Dane Cameron?"

"Yes, it is."

"I'm Dr. Rick Morris at Baybride University in Connecticut."

The university had a renowned teaching hospital. "What can I do for you?" Dane asked.

"I could beat around the bush, but your time is

valuable, as is mine, so I'll get straight to the point. I'm hoping you'll accept a position at our university.''

Dane was taken aback for a moment. Knowing the screening process necessary at most institutions, he finally responded, ''I didn't apply for one.''

''No, you didn't,'' Dr. Morris agreed. ''But the truth is—we're understaffed. And we know your reputation. I also know about your accident, your consulting work and your leaving your specialty. Baybride has done its homework. We feel you would be an asset to our teaching staff. Is performing surgery still out of the question for you?''

''I've just begun physical therapy. I postponed doing it after the accident. Some of the mobility has returned to my fingers, but I'm still not sure of the prognosis.''

With a grunt of dismissal, Morris said easily, ''We can have one of our experts check you out. But whether you can perform surgery or not, we want you here. Is that within the realm of possibility?''

After a phone conversation that had turned into a persuasive advertisement explaining everything Baybride could offer Dane, he drove to the high school, thinking about what Dr. Morris had said. *We want you here. Is that within the realm of possibility?*

What was within the realm of possibility today might not have been possible two months ago. Or two weeks ago. A position at a prestigious university like Baybride wasn't an offer to be taken lightly. He wouldn't just be doing consulting work, he'd actually be teaching young doctors everything he knew. There was an excitement in that. Besides that, Dr. Morris had detailed every advantage of the physical therapy unit at Baybride's Hospital. If anyone could help

Dane recover full use of his hand, the physical therapists there could.

It was a lot to think about…a very tempting offer.

But then Dane thought about Maria and the kind of life he'd found in Red Bluff, so different from back East.

He'd told Dr. Morris he'd contact him by the end of next week. That would give him time to weigh the pros and cons, to figure out the direction of his future.

Red Bluff's high school teemed with the activity of teenagers. Dane checked in at the office and then went to the gym. Finding the coach outside supervising practice drills, Dane was about to alert him that he was ready to start when he caught sight of a group of boys under the overhang of the building. He sensed more was going on than a friendly discussion. Joe Eagle stood toe-to-toe with a tall, lean, russet-haired teenager—Trevor, Dane guessed. The boy's expression looked ready for trouble. The others in the circle seemed to be egging on both boys.

Dane thought about alerting the coach and letting him handle it. He thought about stepping in himself. Instead of doing either, he watched closely, ready to move if he had to. He wanted to see how Joe was going to handle this. Although Maria's brother still eyed him cautiously at times, the wariness was gone.

As Dane watched the teenagers under the overhang, the taller boy gave Joe a shove. Joe looked angry, but he stood still and didn't raise his fists.

Trevor sneered, "Afraid to fight, Indian? I thought your kind was real good at that."

When Joe didn't react, it seemed to make the boy even angrier and his fist shot out.

Dane took a step forward.

But then, using one of the moves Dane had taught him, Joe side-stepped and the boy swung into the air.

Dane had to smile to himself, thinking, *Good job, Joe.*

Trevor looked surprised, mad as hell, and went after Joe again. But in a move that said Joe had been practicing, the teenager stepped out of harm's way and tripped the other boy easily. The kid landed on his butt with a thump.

As Joe stood over him, he said, "If you want to fight, I'll fight. But that's not going to solve anything. I'm proud of being Cheyenne. Do you have any pride about where you came from?"

The other boys were looking at Joe differently now...with respect.

Joe's opponent stood and brushed himself off, mumbling something Dane couldn't hear.

"You probably don't even know who your ancestors are," Joe went on. "Why don't you go look them up? And if they came over on the Mayflower, just remember the Cheyenne were here first."

Turning away from the group, Joe saw Dane. His face reddened and then just looked self-satisfied. Crossing to him, Joe said, "I guess you heard that."

"I *saw* that. You were good."

"I just used what you showed me."

After a few moments of awkward silence, Joe added, "Thanks for not interfering."

"I was ready to yell for the coach," Dane admitted. "But I also know every man has to learn how to fight his own battles."

With a half smile and a sideways glance, Joe shrugged. Then he muttered, "I guess it's okay if you have a thing for my sister. I won't have to worry about her so much anymore.''

A thing for Maria. A job offer back East. Acceptance from an Eagle. Dane had to be honest. ''I don't know what's going to happen with your sister. Both of our lives are pretty complicated.''

After Joe studied Dane for a few moments, he shrugged again. ''At least you're up-front about it. Tony was an s.o.b., leaving her like that.''

Dane agreed. But he might be leaving Maria, too. If he did, it would put him in the same category as Tony Youngbear. He didn't like that idea at all.

After Dane finished at the high school, he stopped at the town deli and bought a variety of sandwiches, bags of chips and an assortment of sodas. Maria and Joan usually brought yogurt or salad for lunch, but he figured they might like a change. Betsy usually went out for her hour lunch break.

Betsy had already left when he returned to the clinic. Joan told him that Maria was seeing her last patient for the morning. He set all the food he'd bought on the desk in the office. When he asked Joan for her preference in sandwiches, she shook her head. ''I've got to run a few errands. You and Maria enjoy them.''

After Maria finished with her last patient, she came into the office and saw the food and drinks on the coffee table in front of the sofa. ''What's this?''

''I thought you might like lunch.''

She laughed. ''It looks like someone was hungry. How'd the physicals go?''

''Fine. I have two more classes to do next week.''

If Joe wanted to tell her what had happened, he would.

Maria took off her lab coat and hung it on her chair. "Clara called to thank us again. Virgil's already giving her a mess of trouble, arguing with her about what he can and can't eat. I told her to add cayenne pepper and lots of garlic to his chicken and turkey. Then he won't complain that it's tasteless."

"You're all heart," Dane said with a smile.

Then his smile faded because he knew Maria *was* all heart, and he had to tell her about that phone call he'd received. As Maria walked to the sofa, Dane appreciated every graceful move, the vitality in her step, the smile on her lips.

After she sat down beside him, she picked up a turkey sandwich. "Looks great."

But he didn't want to talk about the food. "I got a phone call this morning."

She turned curious eyes on him. "From?"

"Baybride University in Connecticut. They want me to accept a teaching position. If I can eventually perform surgery, they want me on staff at the hospital."

"I see," she said slowly, laying her sandwich back down on the table. "I knew you'd leave... eventually."

"I didn't say I was leaving."

She tilted her head. "But you're considering it."

"I'd be a fool not to."

And I'd be a fool to ask you to stay, Maria thought sadly. She loved Dane with all her heart, and she desperately wanted him to stay. But she couldn't tell him how she felt. It was much too soon for him. And she wouldn't ask him to stay. She'd practically begged Tony to stay, and he'd still left her. They'd even had marriage vows between them.

If Dane felt anything for her, wouldn't he ask her to go with him? The thought gave her a lilting hope that amazed her. Would she consider it? If Dane loved her, she'd consider anything. That scared her almost as much as her feelings for him.

And suddenly she couldn't sit here beside him like this, their elbows brushing, their knees grazing, their eyes meeting. Too many jumbled feelings were rolling over themselves inside of her, and there was no way she could swallow a bite of that turkey sandwich.

Quickly she stood.

"What's the matter?" he asked.

"I just remembered I have some errands to run, too. I won't have time to eat lunch."

"Maria…"

She wasn't going to listen to his protest. She wasn't going to help him decide whether to stay or go. Right now she needed to get away from him and her feelings for him.

Taking her purse from the bottom right drawer of her desk, she said, "See you in about an hour," and then flew out the door.

Dane Cameron would be driving into the sunset without her, and she had to get used to the idea.

When Dane pulled into the self-serve gas station on Saturday evening, he parked behind a pick-up truck at the pump in front of him. It wasn't until he got out that he saw Jase McGraw putting the nozzle for the gasoline back in its holder. He raised his hand in salute, and Jase walked over to him.

The sheriff was out of uniform, dressed in jeans

and a T-shirt, like Dane. "How are you doing?" Jase asked amiably.

He'd spoken with Jase and Allison for a while at Frank Nightwalker's party. He'd liked them both. "Besides filling up the tank, I should probably go to the car wash," he said in a wry tone. Although Joe had washed and waxed his SUV last Saturday, the car was grimy again.

"I know what you mean. I don't think there's anyplace dustier than Red Bluff when it hasn't rained in a month. I heard there's a front moving in, but we need more than thunderstorms that are going to cause flash floods."

Dane realized it hadn't rained since he'd arrived in the town. "How's the new baby?" he asked, continuing the small talk, needing a distraction from going back to his apartment and thinking about Maria.

Since she'd left their office in such a hurry, she'd avoided him. He couldn't blame her. Until he decided whether he was staying or going, it would hurt to be with her. But even if he stayed, he didn't know what would happen. She wanted so much. The idea of starting over, the possibility of risking giving his life to another person again and then having everything snatched away, wasn't even something he wanted to consider.

Jase slid one hand into his jeans pocket. "Elizabeth is doing just fine. In fact, she has two women fussing over her about now. Maria came over with Sunny."

"I see." He'd seen Maria and Sunny leave earlier and thought they might be going to her parents' ranch. He had to make the decision whether he was going to that anniversary party tomorrow or not.

"In fact," Jase said casually, "Maria told us you might be leaving."

"I had a job offer."

"That's a shame. I mean for us. The people here seem to like you. They don't always accept outsiders easily."

Remembering his conversation with Jase at Frank Nightwalker's party, Dane recalled that the sheriff had moved to Red Bluff from Richmond about seven years ago. "Did you feel like an outsider when you moved here?"

"Sure did. But I just did my job, and soon people respected that."

"Everything seems to have worked out well for you."

"It has. I liked it here before Allison came. Since we got married, there's no place else I'd rather be."

"You knew her before?" Dane recalled what Frank had said about Allison visiting Jase.

"Oh, yeah," he said. "She was my best friend's wife. But Dave was killed in the line of duty, and Allison found out some things she hadn't known about him. She came out here to get away from Richmond and everything that had happened."

"And you connected."

"You could say that."

Dane assumed that was an understatement. He'd seen Jase and Allison together. They acted as if they could hardly bear to be separated from each other even after almost three years of marriage. "I like Red Bluff," he said.

"But not enough to stay." Jase's look was probing.

"It's complicated."

"I imagine it might be. I know Maria pretty well.

She was upset today about something. Although she didn't come right out and say it, I think her problem has a lot to do with you."

Dane couldn't help but hear the protective note in Jase's voice.

When he remained silent, Jase went on. "Maria hasn't let herself care about a man since her husband divorced her. When I saw you two dancing the other night at Frank's, I got the feeling that had changed."

"I never meant to hurt her," Dane said. "I never meant to get involved at all."

"I told myself that same thing when Allison arrived in Red Bluff."

"But you didn't hurt her."

"I almost did. And she almost left without ever knowing how I really felt about her."

After a few silent moments Dane admitted, "I came here with a lot of baggage."

Jase smiled. "Oh, I know baggage. I carried it around and used it as an excuse until I practically lost Allison. Then I realized that nothing was more important than the two of us being together." Shrugging, he added, "But my life isn't yours." He extended his hand. "I wish you luck in whatever you decide to do."

After church on Sunday morning, Maria tried to keep her mind on her parents' anniversary party and everything she was supposed to take. She had all of it in the car. But her mind kept wandering back to Dane and the decision he was going to make. She'd gone to Allison's last night to talk to her about it, knowing that Allison knew what it was like to be in love and think it wasn't going to work out. She and

Jase had gone through rough patches before they'd really found each other. Maria hadn't realized her involvement in all of that until a few months after the wedding, when she and Allison had gone to lunch together. By then Allison was working with her at the clinic. Bonds of friendship had formed that made confidences easy.

But last night Allison hadn't had any advice for her. This situation was different. Maria could tell Dane her feelings. But that might make his choices even more difficult. She wanted him to stay, but she wanted him to be happy. And as far as her going with him...that invitation had to come from him.

It was all so confusing. She didn't know if he was going to be at the party this afternoon. If he was, she'd have to keep her distance. It hurt too much to be near him.

The bright sunlight on the terrace was like a balm, and Maria opened the door and the screen. But before she could even take a breath, Sunny had slipped around her legs and scurried outside. Maria always marveled at the quickness of her two-year-old.

This morning, though, she didn't appreciate it. Before Maria could call her daughter's name or catch her, Sunny was running over to Dane's terrace and standing at his glass door, tapping on it.

Maria groaned inwardly. Just what she didn't need.

When Dane came to the door, he saw Sunny and smiled. But then his gaze met Maria's and his expression became serious.

Opening the door, he concentrated on her daughter. "And what can I do for you this morning?"

"Par-tee. 'Loons."

There was a look in Dane's eyes that told Maria

he hadn't intended to go to the party. But then he looked down at Sunny and gathered her up into his arms. "So you're going to a party with balloons. And I'll bet there will be a cake with icing."

Sunny nodded her head vigorously. "I-cing."

He laughed. "If I come, do I have to get dressed up?"

Maria answered for her daughter in an encouraging voice, knowing it would hurt to be near Dane when she had so little time with him. "It's casual. You can wear whatever you want."

Dane's gaze took in her red-and-white-patterned sundress. She'd worn a white bolero jacket with it this morning to church. But now with the jacket off, she could feel the heat of his eyes on her bare shoulders.

"All right," he said. "I might as well drive. It's silly to take two cars."

"You can drive," Maria agreed, "but we'd better use my car because of the car seat."

His eyes took on that haunted look for a moment, and then he nodded. "What time do you want to leave?"

"The party's at three. But I'm taking a casserole and paper cups, knives and forks. That kind of thing. Is two-thirty okay?"

"That's fine. I'll see you then."

As he went to put Sunny down, she wrapped her little arms around his neck and squeezed tight. "Hug," she demanded in that two-year-old voice that told him she wouldn't be denied.

He gave her a tight hug and swung her in a circle, making her giggle. Then he set her down on the ground. It practically broke Maria's heart to see him with Sunny like this. He would be such a wonderful father.

But fatherhood might be something that hurt too much for Dane to ever try again.

When they drove to her parents' ranch later that afternoon, Dane seemed so far away from her. It was as if he was already gone. As soon as they were in the house, Sunny went to help one of her aunts, who was tying helium balloons outside on the patio. Dane stopped to talk to Maria's father, and his manner was casual. But Maria sensed tension in him and didn't know how much he was going to enjoy a party atmosphere. She knew he was good at masking his feelings, at masking his pain. She knew about masking pain. But she also knew that at some point you had to let it go. Letting go always seemed much harder than holding on.

She was readying a dish of guacamole when Dane came back into the kitchen. "I told your Dad I'd get us something to drink."

She moved toward the refrigerator at the same time he did, and they almost collided. He caught her by her elbows and his hands on her skin were hot. The desire in his eyes was intense, and she thought he might kiss her. She thought she might not care what they did, right here in her parents' kitchen.

But then Dane quickly released her and stepped back. His jaw was set firmly, and she knew there was nothing they could say to each other. That hurt. All she wanted to do was plead with him to stay. But she couldn't do that. It wasn't only her pride. That had been the problem with Tony. What if her husband had stayed when he really would rather have gone? What kind of marriage would they have had?

No. Dane had to make this decision on his own.

"There's lemonade in the refrigerator," she said, turning away from him and opening the door.

When he moved to the other side of the table and reached for two plastic cups, she knew this afternoon was going to be the end of whatever was between them. She knew it as surely as the fact the sun would set tonight and she'd be alone in her bedroom, wishing she wasn't.

The festivities of the afternoon swept Maria along with them. She'd known what her sisters and brothers were planning and had looked forward to today. But the sadness in her heart kept weighing her down. And the tension between her and Dane was like a live wire everyone could feel. She could tell by the looks she was getting from her mom and her dad.

The sun began slipping behind clouds when her sister Rita and her husband Cole presented the Eagles with a collage of pictures from their first anniversary to their thirty-fifth. Then her brother Doug asked his father to open a present from all of them—a silver tray engraved with the anniversary dates as well as the names of all of their children and grandchildren.

Finally Maria gave her mother an envelope and said, "This is from all of us, too."

When Carmella opened it, tears slipped down her cheeks. "We're going on a cruise, Tom," she said to her husband. "Seven whole days." But then she looked up at Maria. "Who's going to take care of the ranch?"

Doug explained, "That's why you have kids, Mom. We're going to take turns staying out here. Everything will be taken care of. You and Dad can just go have fun."

There were hugs all around then. And more tears. Maria couldn't help glancing at Dane, whose jaw was set, his shoulders squared and tense. She imagined he was thinking about everything he'd lost—the anniversaries he'd never have…the grandchildren he'd never see.

The other guests presented the Eagles with their presents then. There was much laughter and remembering and talk about their cruise to Mexico and what they'd see there.

The afternoon passed quickly after that, with everyone eating from the bountiful buffet. As the guests enjoyed desserts, gray clouds overtook the blue sky. Thunder rolled a couple of times, and the guests began to leave.

Maria saw Dane disappear into her workshop and supposed he was just putting in time until she was ready to go, too. She'd taken a casserole of beans into the kitchen when Joe hurried in after her. "You and Dane have a fight or something?"

"No," she said shortly.

But her answer didn't faze Joe. "Then why are you two acting like you can't stand to be near each other? I thought you had something going on."

"I can't answer your questions now, Joe," she said with a catch in her voice.

"Hey, sis, what's wrong? I thought he was a decent guy. I thought he was making you really have some fun again."

"He *is* a decent man. But he might not be staying here. He was offered a position at a university back East, and it might be too good to pass up."

"You thinking about going with him?" Joe asked, wide-eyed.

"That hasn't come up."

"But you'd go with him, wouldn't you?"

Her brother's perceptiveness made her take a deep breath, then expel it. "He hasn't asked, so it's not a decision I have to make."

Her brother did something then that was uncharacteristic for him. Acting much older than his years, he squeezed her shoulder. "It'll be okay. I know it will."

Maria held on to that thought as thunder grumbled louder and a bolt of lightning hit somewhere close by. But she didn't know if she believed it.

Chapter Ten

The rain poured down in heavy sheets as Dane drove away from the ranch. Thunder continued to grumble, and lightning streaked across the sky.

Dane glanced over at Maria. She'd been silent ever since she'd gotten into the car. Even before then. She hadn't talked to him since their run-in in the kitchen.

Wondering if thunderstorms bothered Sunny, he checked the rearview mirror. But she was talking to the rag doll she'd taken to her grandmother's. A helium balloon Maria had tied to the door handle bobbed to the ceiling. Sunny had insisted on bringing it with her.

Although Dane had driven this way a few times before, the area looked different now in the grayness and the rain, with water flowing along the sides of the secondary road. The earth was so dry that the downpour was forming streams, running across the road, running over the parched landscape. Bluffs rose on either side of them almost creating a tunnel.

Dane wished he and Maria could talk as they used to. But everything had changed between them.

There was a cleft in the bluff that rose up beside him. Suddenly as he reached it, water flooded through it. It wasn't just a stream of water—it was a river. Surges of it—one after the other—sweeping the car down the road, throwing Dane against the seat belt.

He fought for control. His heart pounded and his grip on the wheel became a stranglehold. But despite his efforts the water swept the car for what seemed like a quarter of a mile. They ended up precariously tilted against a rising bluff.

Dane froze, thinking about another accident at another time and how powerless he had been to control the roll of the car...powerless to prevent the truck from crashing into him. He could feel the roiling of the water against Maria's side of the car. It would only be a matter of minutes until it began seeping under her door. Sunny had started crying, and when he glanced at Maria, she looked paralyzed in her seat.

It only took him a few seconds to decide this time was going to be different. This time he was going to save the woman and child he loved.

He loved.

He *did* love them.

The water rose higher at Maria's door, but his side of the vehicle was lodged on rocks. Rolling down his window, he checked outside and thought there was enough space to get his door open.

Sunny was crying more loudly now and Maria looked terrified. "We'll be trapped in here," she said. "Or else the car will be swept away and we'll drown. That's what happens in these flash floods."

"We're not going to drown," he assured her vehemently, raising his voice over the sound of the rain and rushing water and Sunny's crying. "And we're not going to get swept away. We're going to get out of here and climb up these rocks to safety."

"We can't. Sunny can't."

He unsnapped his seat belt. "I'll take care of Sunny, and I'll take care of you. Just let me see if I can get my door open."

"Dane." His name was a cry of fear and desperation.

Because of the tilt, Maria's side of the car was lower than his. Water was seeping in, and he knew he had to get them all out quickly. "Unfasten your seat belt," he directed her.

"I can't," she said almost in tears.

He could see the fear in her eyes...the knowledge that any movement she made would shift the weight of the car and send it into the rushing water. Instinctively he plucked the cell phone from its cradle on the dash and shoved it into his pocket. Then with his right hand—the hand Maria had tenderly massaged, the hand she convinced him would work again—he grasped her seat belt and managed to release the button. He'd never been more grateful that Maria had convinced him to start physical therapy...grateful that she'd pushed him to begin living again.

"Take my hand," he commanded.

She tried to move toward him, but the steep tilt made it difficult. "Help Sunny first," she pleaded. "Get her out."

"I'm going to get you both out. Trust me, Maria. Take my hand."

Her gaze met his, and he knew she had to make the decision to trust him. He saw the gold sparks in her eyes come alive when she did. As she stretched her arm out, he met her hand with his.

Grasping it firmly, he pulled her toward him. "We can do this, Maria. It might take the two of us to get Sunny to safety, but we can do it."

Jamming his door open as far as it would go, he pulled Maria until she was sitting behind the wheel and he was standing out on the rocks in the pouring rain. She was wearing sandals and he knew this was going to be difficult. But he drew her to him until she was standing beside him.

Then he got back into the car, kneeling on the front seat.

"What are you doing?" she asked, almost in a panic.

"I have to get to Sunny from the front. I'm afraid my weight in the back might push the car into the water. Lean on the hood while I reach back to her. Your weight will help."

The absolute terror in Maria's eyes didn't keep her from doing what he'd asked.

With his long arms he reached into the back and unhooked Sunny's harness. With a little encouragement, she stood on the seat, then came to him willingly. Lifting her between the front headrests, he took a deep breath and handed her out to her mother. Maria gathered her sobbing little girl into her arms and stood with her in the pouring rain.

Then Dane scrambled out. As he did, the car rocked, and he knew it wouldn't be long until it was swept down the road in the wake of the water. He looked up to heaven and said a grateful prayer that they had escaped safely thus far. He could do this.

He could save Maria and Sunny. *And* have a life with them.

Taking Sunny from Maria's arms, he jiggled her a little bit. "We're going to pretend I'm a horse."

Her sobs actually stopped as rain poured down her cheeks. "Horsey?"

"Yep. I'm going to put you up on my shoulders, and I want you to hold on tight. Okay?"

She looked over at her mother for confirmation.

Maria nodded. "I'll be right behind you. We won't let you fall."

Dane gave them both what he hoped was an optimistic smile. Raising his voice to make sure Maria heard him above the sound of the rain and gushing water, he said, "You're going to have to be careful on the rocks...very careful." Then he took off his belt and buckled it around his wrist.

"What are you doing?" she asked.

"I'm giving you a line, and I want you to hold on to it. Tight. No matter what."

"But I'll pull you down."

"No, you won't. We'll be fine. Now come on. It's not that far." They only had about ten feet to climb, but the rocks were large, wet and slick with rain.

With her hair plastered to her head, Maria gazed up at him. He thought he saw love there along with the fear, but he couldn't be sure. After she took hold of the end of the belt, they started. He climbed a rock, balanced himself and Sunny, and then Maria scrambled up beside him.

They did it again and again. She slid once and his breath caught, but he grabbed hold of the belt. Maria held on tight, and he pulled her to safety. Adrenaline was a wonderful thing in an emergency.

Foot after foot they climbed, until finally Dane pulled Maria with him up to the top of the bluff, and they stood panting on the flat surface.

Taking Sunny from his shoulders, he held her in his arms and asked, "Are you okay, little one?"

"Wet," she said matter-of-factly.

He laughed with such relief that Sunny smiled at him.

Then he looked over at Maria as the rain began to let up—from a downpour to a shower. "Are you okay?"

She was as muddy as he was, and it looked as if she'd cut her arm. But she nodded and took Sunny into her arms, hugging her and holding her tight.

Remembering the cell phone, Dane grabbed it from his pocket and called emergency services. Then he put his arm around Maria and Sunny both, adding his heat to theirs, so that they wouldn't get any more chilled.

He wasn't sure how long they stood there like that...how long it was until the shower slowed to a drizzle...until the sky brightened...until the sun came out and shone in its glory. Releasing Maria and Sunny, he went to the edge of the crest and looked over. The car had indeed been swept from the rocks down the road about forty yards and was now almost submerged. He didn't want Maria to see it. He didn't want her to realize how close they'd come to losing each other and Sunny.

Dane could see that Maria was trembling as she sat on a large boulder, Sunny on her lap, lifting her face to the brightening sky. He couldn't tell if there were tears on her cheeks or if the wetness was streaks of rain. There was so much he wanted to say to her. But not here. Not like this. It was more important they keep Sunny from being frightened until help arrived.

With the sun shining through the rain, a double rainbow appeared in the sky. Dane pointed it out to Sunny and took it as an omen. There was no doubt in his mind what decision about his career would be the right one to make.

When he heard the sound of an engine, he went to the other side of the mesa and saw a black Jeep coming up a less-traveled road, one not covered with water. They could have attempted climbing down, but he knew it was better if they waited for help with ropes and extra hands. When he saw who the help was, he smiled. It was Jase McGraw and Wyatt Baumgardner.

With harnesses and ropes, the sheriff and his deputy climbed up the back of the cliff. Once he and Wyatt reached them, Jase took one look at their muddy clothes and their rain-soaked hair and said, "I'm afraid to ask where your car is."

Dane pointed, but then shook his head, warning Jase he didn't want to make an issue of it.

Jase must have gotten the message because he put his hand on Maria's shoulder. "Are you okay?"

She just nodded.

Jase held out his arms to Sunny. "I have a little swing to put you into. That'll make it easier for us to carry you down this big hill. How about it?"

"Swing?" Sunny asked.

"Well, not exactly a swing," he admitted. "But it'll keep you safe on my back until we get to the bottom of the hill. Okay?"

Again Sunny looked to her mom.

Maria managed, "We're coming, too. Jase'll give you a nice ride like Dane did."

At that the uncertainty left Sunny's face and she smiled.

Maria wouldn't meet Dane's gaze, and he wondered why. Maybe it was too late to tell her everything in his heart. Maybe it was too late to tell her that she and Sunny had become his life. Maybe it was too late to tell her that, faced with losing them, he'd realized what love really meant. It meant taking the risk of giving his heart again...giving it completely to a woman and child who could become his world. It meant putting fear and the past behind him and having the courage to reach out to Maria to find happiness again.

About forty-five minutes later, Jase and Wyatt dropped them off at their apartment building. Maria thanked both lawmen with hugs, and Dane added his gratitude, shaking the men's hands. Then they walked silently to their apartments. Maria was holding on to Sunny, still wrapped in the blanket Jase had provided, as if she'd never let her go. Dane understood exactly how she felt.

As they passed his door, he asked her, "Do you need help with Sunny?"

But Maria shook her head. "We'll both get in the shower and warm up. Then we'll be fine."

"As soon as I get a shower, I'll be over. We have to talk."

"Dane, this isn't a good time..."

"We have to talk, Maria. It'll only take me ten minutes to clean up. Do you want to give me your key so I don't have to disturb you if you're not dressed yet?"

She looked at him oddly, unlocked her door, then handed him the key. Her fingers were cold when they touched his.

"I have a bottle of brandy. I'll bring it over with me."

Still she didn't speak but went inside her apartment.

Fifteen minutes later Dane was sitting in Maria's living room, waiting for her, the bottle of brandy and two glasses on the coffee table. Restless, he stood and paced, unsure how to approach her, unsure of exactly what to say.

Finally he heard her footsteps as she came into the living room. "Sunny fell asleep already," she said softly. Then Maria slowly crossed to him.

She'd washed and dried her hair, and it was silky and loose. She'd also pulled on a white knit top and yellow shorts. Sometimes he couldn't believe how much she brightened up his life...brightened up his world...brightened up his future.

Tilting her chin up, Maria fortified herself for what was to come. She had seen Dane's face that moment in the car when he'd realized what kind of predicament they were in. It had held so much turmoil. It was as if he'd been reliving his accident. She and Sunny were a burden he didn't want...he didn't need. It wasn't just a matter of him being ready for love again. He didn't want the responsibility for someone else's happiness...for someone else's life. What had happened to them this afternoon had made that particularly clear.

When they'd climbed to the top of the bluff, there had been such relief on his face. His silence since then had convinced her he was going to tell her he was leaving Red Bluff.

And there was nothing she could do about it. He needed freedom to heal, and she was going to give him that.

Because she loved him.

"Thank you for saving us," she said. On the last word her voice broke, and she knew tears glistened in her eyes.

Instead of backing away as she suspected he might, he wiped her tears from her cheek with his thumb.

Maria stilled, and her breath almost stopped. She had braced herself for this confrontation with Dane and the words that would tell her he was leaving her life.

When he dropped his hand to his side, his expression was so serious she wanted to run. But then he started speaking. "I couldn't lose you and Sunny. I *won't* lose you and Sunny. I've been a fool to think I could leave you."

It took her a few moments to finally realize what he'd said. She was afraid she'd misunderstood. "What about Baybride? What about your career?"

Her heart pounded at least three times until he answered, "My career means nothing compared to the love I feel for you and Sunny. Will you marry me?"

For the first time in her life, Maria was overcome and couldn't answer.

At her expression Dane laughed and took her hands in his. "I've never seen you speechless before."

Maybe it was the sound of his laughter, maybe it was the love she saw in his eyes that got through to her, that warmed her in ways the hot shower hadn't, that filled her with so much happiness she thought she'd burst with it. Grateful he had saved them this afternoon, joy-filled and thankful and loving him more than she had ever loved anyone except Sunny, she retorted, "I might be speechless, but I know how to give you an answer."

Pulling her hands from his, she raised herself on tiptoe, wrapped her arms around his neck and put her lips on his.

Dane enfolded her in his arms, kissing her with all the depth of his passion and love.

But then she pulled back, needing to be certain that Dane was doing what would make him truly happy. "Are you sure you want to stay in Red Bluff? You're giving up so much."

Clasping her hand, he pulled her with him to the sofa and sat with his arm around her, his chin on her hair. "I won't be giving up anything. I like working at the clinic. I'll keep up with the physical therapy here, either with you or in Albuquerque. If I can get my hand back to 100 percent, I can look into performing surgery again in Albuquerque."

"I can't believe you're willing to do that," she murmured. "I want you to know…you don't have to. I'll go with you anyplace you want to go." And she absolutely meant it. Dane was her road and her ballast and her future. She could go anywhere with him and make a home for the three of them. Yes, she loved her family and she needed them, too. But if she had to choose, she would choose to be with Dane.

He tightened his arm around her. "There's no place I'd rather be. I've found a home here, and I think in time your family might accept me, too."

"You're already part of my family. Joe thinks

you're a decent guy. And Mom and Dad? They know I love you. They'll want whatever makes me happy.''

"*You* make me happy,'' Dane assured her, as he scooped her onto his lap and claimed her lips with the fervor of a man in love...a man who wanted to spend a lifetime with a woman.

Maria returned Dane's desire, promising her heart and soul. Promising a lifetime of love.

The sun hung suspended between day and dusk, showering the sky with golden rays that streaked into pink and orange, purple and blue. The four-piece band on the Eagles' patio began a slow, sentimental melody as Dane took Maria in his arms for their wedding dance. He'd never seen her look more beautiful than she did in the white satin and lace gown. And she was his.

As friends and family looked on, enjoying the remains of their wedding cake, Maria gazed up at him with her beautiful brown eyes. "I almost wish today would never end.''

"But if today didn't end, we wouldn't have tonight," he said simply.

It was the middle of October and they'd decided to wait until their wedding night to consummate their love. The past two months had been busy with planning and preparations and details for the wedding that had taken place at the small Catholic church in Red Bluff. They'd decided to have the reception here at Maria's parents' ranch, not only because it pleased Carmella and Tom, but because it seemed so very appropriate.

But through each minute they'd spent planning everything, they'd longed to become truly one.

Tonight they would.

"My family wanted to know exactly where we were staying in Albuquerque," Maria said with a mischievous smile. "But I wouldn't tell them. They have our pager numbers. I told Mama if there was an emergency, she could reach us through them."

Dane laughed. "One night isn't much of a honeymoon," he admitted.

They'd found a doctor in Albuquerque to cover the clinic for today and tomorrow. But they couldn't be away longer than that.

"Tonight is just the beginning of our honeymoon," Maria said softly with a smile that promised him every night of their lives. But then she added, "I'm so happy, I'm almost afraid."

He pulled her closer. "You don't *ever* have to be afraid. Not as long as we're together. Have I told you how grateful I am to you? When I came to Red Bluff, I was lost. You helped me find myself again, as well as you. I love you, Maria. And tonight I'm going to show you exactly how much."

Then, in spite of family and friends watching, Maria slid her arms around Dane's neck and kissed him. Holding her as if he'd never let her go, he claimed her as his wife, as their wedding guests looked on and began applauding.

Epilogue

One Year Later

The fire leaped brightly in the brick fireplace of the rambling ranch house. Dane stood before the rough-hewn mantel, his arm around Maria, facing their friends and Maria's family, who had also become *his* family. He and Maria and Sunny had moved into their new house two weeks ago. It had three bedrooms, a large kitchen, a family room with a fold-out sofa bed for any guests who might want to stay overnight, and a screened back porch that was already one of their favorite spots. Everyone had taken the grand tour, and now Dane had called them all together before they shared snacks and stories and laughter from their week and their lives.

"Maria and I want to share our good news with you," he said with a broad smile, curving his arm around his wife's waist and drawing her close.

She was wearing a long-sleeved turquoise blouse and jeans and had worn her hair loose, the way he liked it.

"We have an announcement to make," he continued. "We're going to have a baby."

Joe let out a cheer as Maria's mom came to hug her, and her dad shook Dane's hand. Everyone wished them well, and a few warned them about sleepless nights.

But then Jase McGraw added, "It's all worth it."

Dane had already had a taste of fatherhood again. Sunny brought him so much joy he could hardly believe how fortunate he was.

As relatives and friends eventually moved into the kitchen to sample the food, Maria looked up at him. "Since you're working at the hospital now, as well as at the clinic, we'd better start looking for a new doctor to replace me."

They hadn't specifically talked about this yet. "A temporary doctor?"

"Maybe more than temporary. I'd like to stay home for a while after the baby's born. Do you think we can swing it?"

He enfolded her in his arms. "Sure, we can swing it. Actually I love the idea of you being home with our children. Soon I'll officially be Sunny's father." The adoption process was well on its way.

"That was the best idea you had, other than asking me to marry you," Maria teased.

As he laughed, Sunny came running to him from the kitchen. She held out her arms to him and he scooped her up. While he held his daughter with one arm, he hugged Maria to him with the other, knowing he was the most fortunate man in all the world. His move to Red Bluff had brought him all of his heart's desires—a woman to share nights of passion and days of loving, a daughter who blessed their lives with sunshine and laughter, and now a new baby who would be a tangible symbol of his and Maria's spiritual, emotional and physical bond.

Maria gazed up at him with everything she felt. "I love you, Dane Cameron."

"And I love you, Maria Cameron. Forever and always."

The fire burned brightly, ever changing, as Dane kissed his wife, hearing the murmur of voices from the people they loved in the kitchen. He'd left the past behind—not forgetting it, but cherishing it. His gift, in return for letting go of his old life, was the opening of his heart to a new one.

When he lifted his head and gazed down at his wife, he suggested, "Let's join our company in the kitchen."

She nodded, and they walked hand in hand and heart-to-heart into the life they were creating from the bounty of their love.

* * * * *

Don't miss
Karen Rose Smith's next book,
HIS LITTLE GIRL'S LAUGHTER,

available October 2001
from Silhouette Special Edition.

MAITLAND MATERNITY

You loved
the Maitland
family. Now meet
the long-lost Maitlands...!

In August 2001, Marie Ferrarella introduces
Rafe Maitland, a rugged rancher with a little girl he'd
do anything to keep, including—*gulp!*—get married,
in **THE INHERITANCE**, a specially packaged story!

Look for it near Silhouette and Harlequin's single titles!

**Then meet Rafe's siblings in
Silhouette Romance® in the coming months:**

Myrna Mackenzie continues the story
of the Maitlands with prodigal
daughter Laura Maitland in
September 2001's
A VERY SPECIAL DELIVERY.

October 2001 brings
the conclusion to this
spin-off of the popular
Maitland family series, reuniting
black sheep Luke Maitland with
his family in Stella Bagwell's
THE MISSING MAITLAND.

Available at your favorite retail outlet.

Silhouette®
Where love comes alive™

Visit Silhouette at www.eHarlequin.com   SRMAIT1

Feel like a star with Silhouette.

We will fly you and a guest to New York City for an exciting weekend stay at a glamorous 5-star hotel. Experience a refreshing day at one of New York's trendiest spas and have your photo taken by a professional. Plus, receive $1,000 U.S. spending money!

Flowers...long walks...dinner for two... how does Silhouette Books make romance come alive for you?

Send us a script, with 500 words or less, along with visuals (only drawings, magazine cutouts or photographs or combination thereof). Show us how Silhouette Makes Your Love Come Alive. Be creative and have fun. No purchase necessary. All entries must be clearly marked with your name, address and telephone number. All entries will become property of Silhouette and are not returnable. **Contest closes September 28, 2001.**

Please send your entry to: **Silhouette Makes You a Star!**

In U.S.A.
P.O. Box 9069
Buffalo, NY, 14269-9069

In Canada
P.O. Box 637
Fort Erie, ON, L2A 5X3

Look for contest details on the next page, by visiting www.eHarlequin.com or request a copy by sending a self-addressed envelope to the applicable address above. Contest open to Canadian and U.S. residents who are 18 or over. Void where prohibited.

Our lucky winner's photo will appear in a Silhouette ad. Join the fun!

SRMYAS1

HARLEQUIN "SILHOUETTE MAKES YOU A STAR!" CONTEST 1308
OFFICIAL RULES
NO PURCHASE NECESSARY TO ENTER

1. To enter, follow directions published in the offer to which you are responding. Contest begins June 1, 2001, and ends on September 28, 2001. Entries must be postmarked by September 28, 2001, and received by October 5, 2001. Enter by hand-printing (or typing) on an 8 ½" x 11" piece of paper your name, address (including zip code), contest number/name and attaching a script containing 500 words or less, along with drawings, photographs or magazine cutouts, or combinations thereof (i.e., collage) on no larger than 9" x 12" piece of paper, describing how the Silhouette books make romance come alive for you. Mail via first-class mail to: Harlequin "Silhouette Makes You a Star!" Contest 1308, (in the U.S.) P.O. Box 9069, Buffalo, NY 14269-9069, (in Canada) P.O. Box 637, Fort Erie, Ontario, Canada L2A 5X3. Limit one entry per person, household or organization.

2. Contests will be judged by a panel of members of the Harlequin editorial, marketing and public relations staff. Fifty percent of criteria will be judged against script and fifty percent will be judged against drawing, photographs and/or magazine cutouts. Judging criteria will be based on the following:

   - Sincerity—25%
   - Originality and Creativity—50%
   - Emotionally Compelling—25%

   In the event of a tie, duplicate prizes will be awarded. Decisions of the judges are final.

3. All entries become the property of Torstar Corp. and may be used for future promotional purposes. Entries will not be returned. No responsibility is assumed for lost, late, illegible, incomplete, inaccurate, nondelivered or misdirected mail.

4. Contest open only to residents of the U.S. (except Puerto Rico) and Canada who are 18 years of age or older, and is void wherever prohibited by law; all applicable laws and regulations apply. Any litigation within the Province of Quebec respecting the conduct or organization of a publicity contest may be submitted to the Régie des alcools, des courses et des jeux for a ruling. Any litigation respecting the awarding of a prize may be submitted to the Régie des alcools, des courses et des jeux only for the purpose of helping the parties reach a settlement. Employees and immediate family members of Torstar Corp. and D. L. Blair, Inc., their affiliates, subsidiaries and all other agencies, entities and persons connected with the use, marketing or conduct of this contest are not eligible to enter. Taxes on prizes are the sole responsibility of winner. Acceptance of any prize offered constitutes permission to use winner's name, photograph or other likeness for the purposes of advertising, trade and promotion on behalf of Torstar Corp., its affiliates and subsidiaries without further compensation to the winner, unless prohibited by law.

5. Winner will be determined no later than November 30, 2001, and will be notified by mail. Winner will be required to sign and return an Affidavit of Eligibility/Release of Liability/Publicity Release form within 15 days after winner notification. Noncompliance within that time period may result in disqualification and an alternative winner may be selected. All travelers must execute a Release of Liability prior to ticketing and must possess required travel documents (e.g., passport, photo ID) where applicable. Trip must be booked by December 31, 2001, and completed within one year of notification. No substitution of prize permitted by winner. Torstar Corp. and D. L. Blair, Inc., their parents, affiliates and subsidiaries are not responsible for errors in printing of contest, entries and/or game pieces. In the event of printing or other errors that may result in unintended prize values or duplication of prizes, all affected game pieces or entries shall be null and void. **Purchase or acceptance of a product offer does not improve your chances of winning.**

6. Prizes: (1) Grand Prize—A 2-night/3-day trip for two (2) to New York City, including round-trip coach air transportation nearest winner's home and hotel accommodations (double occupancy) at The Plaza Hotel, a glamorous afternoon makeover at a trendy New York spa, $1,000 in U.S. spending money and an opportunity to have a professional photo taken and appear in a Silhouette advertisement (approximate retail value: $7,000). (10) Ten Runner-Up Prizes of gift packages (retail value $50 ea.). Prizes consist of only those items listed as part of the prize. Limit one prize per person. Prize is valued in U.S. currency.

7. For the name of the winner (available after December 31, 2001) send a self-addressed, stamped envelope to: Harlequin "Silhouette Makes You a Star!" Contest 1197 Winners, P.O. Box 4200 Blair, NE 68009-4200 or you may access the www.eHarlequin.com Web site through February 28, 2002.

Contest sponsored by Torstar Corp., P.O. Box 9042, Buffalo, NY 14269-9042.

SRMYAS2

If you enjoyed what you just read,
then we've got an offer you can't resist!

Take 2 bestselling love stories FREE!

Plus get a FREE surprise gift!